The **FUN STARTS HERE!**

Four Favorite Chapter Books in One

A STEPPING STONE BOOK™

Random House  New York

All rights reserved. Published in the United States by Random House Children's Books, a division of Penguin Random House LLC, New York.

Random House and the colophon and A to Z Mysteries are registered trademarks and A Stepping Stone Book and the colophon and the A to Z Mysteries colophon are trademarks of Penguin Random House LLC. Magic Tree House is a registered trademark of Mary Pope Osborne, used under license. Junie B. Jones is a registered trademark of Barbara Park, used under license. PURRMAIDS® is a registered trademark of KIKIDOODLE LLC and is used under license from KIKIDOODLE LLC.

The works that appear herein were originally published separately in the United States by Random House Children's Books, a division of Penguin Random House LLC, New York.

Visit us on the Web!
rhcbooks.com
MagicTreeHouse.com
JunieBJones.com

Educators and librarians, for a variety of teaching tools, visit us at RHTeachersLibrarians.com

The Library of Congress has catalogued the individual books under the following Control Numbers: 91051106 (*Dinosaurs Before Dark*), 91051104 (*Junie B. Jones and the Stupid Smelly Bus*), 97002030 (*The Absent Author*), 2016033947 (*The Scaredy Cat*).

ISBN 978-1-9848-3059-3

Printed in the United States of America
10 9 8 7 6 5 4 3 2 1

First Edition

These books have been officially leveled by using the F&P Text Level Gradient™ Leveling System.

Random House Children's Books supports the First Amendment and celebrates the right to read.

CONTENTS

MARY POPE OSBORNE

MAGIC TREE HOUSE®

#1 Dinosaurs Before Dark

Magic Tree House®

For a list of Magic Tree House® Merlin Missions and other
Magic Tree House® titles, visit MagicTreeHouse.com.

MAGIC TREE HOUSE®

#1 DINOSAURS BEFORE DARK

BY MARY POPE OSBORNE
ILLUSTRATED BY SAL MURDOCCA

A STEPPING STONE BOOK™

Random House 🏠 New York

Contents

CHAPTER ONE

INTO THE WOODS

"Help! A monster!" said Annie.

"Yeah, sure," said Jack. "A real monster in Frog Creek, Pennsylvania."

"Run, Jack!" said Annie. She ran up the road.

Oh, brother, thought Jack. This is what he got for spending time with his seven-year-old sister.

Annie loved pretend stuff. But Jack was eight and a half. He liked *real* things.

"Watch out, Jack! The monster's coming!" said Annie.

Jack didn't say anything.

"Come on, Jack, I'll race you!" said Annie.

"No, thanks," said Jack.

Annie raced alone into the woods.

Jack looked at the sky. The sun was about to set.

"Come on, Annie! It's time to go home!" yelled Jack.

But Annie didn't answer.

Jack waited.

"Annie!" he called again.

"Jack! Jack!" Annie shouted. "Come here! Quick!"

Jack groaned. "This better be good," he said.

Jack left the road and headed into the woods. The trees were lit with a golden late-afternoon light.

"Over here!" called Annie.

Annie was standing under a tall oak tree. "Look!" she said. She pointed at a rope ladder. It was hanging down from high in the tree.

"Wow," Jack whispered.

At the top of the tree was a tree house, tucked between two branches.

"That must be the highest tree house in the world," said Annie.

"Who built it?" asked Jack. "I've never seen it before."

"I don't know. But I'm going up," said Annie.

"No! We don't know who it belongs to," said Jack.

"Just for a teeny minute," said Annie. She started up the ladder.

"Annie, come back!" said Jack.

But Annie kept climbing. She climbed all the way up to the tallest branches.

Jack sighed. "Annie, it's almost dark! We have to go home!"

Annie disappeared inside the tree house.

"Annie!" Jack called.

Jack waited a moment. He was about to call again when Annie poked her head out of the tree house window.

"Books!" Annie shouted.

"What?" Jack said.

"It's filled with books!" said Annie.

Oh, man! Jack thought. He loved books.

Jack pushed his glasses into place. He gripped the sides of the rope ladder and started up.

CHAPTER TWO

THE MONSTER

Jack crawled into the tree house.

"Wow," he said. The tree house *was* filled with books. Books were everywhere—very old books with dusty covers and new books with shiny, bright covers.

"Look," said Annie. "You can see far away." She was peering out the tree house window.

Jack looked out the window with her. Below were the tops of the other trees. In the distance he could see the Frog Creek library and the elementary school and the park.

Annie pointed in the other direction.

"There's our house," she said.

Annie was right. Jack could see their white wooden house with its green porch. In the yard next door was their neighbor's black dog, Henry. He looked very tiny.

"Hi, Henry!" shouted Annie.

"Shush! We're not supposed to be up here," said Jack.

Jack glanced around the tree house again. He noticed that bookmarks were sticking out of many of the books. "I wonder who owns all these books," he said.

"I like this one," said Annie. She picked up a book with a castle on the cover.

"Here's a book about Pennsylvania," said Jack. He turned to the page with the bookmark.

"Hey, here's a picture of Frog Creek," said

Jack. "It's a picture of *these* woods!"

"Oh, here's a book for you," said Annie. She held up a book about dinosaurs. A blue silk bookmark was sticking out of it.

"Let me see," said Jack. He set his backpack down on the floor and grabbed the book from Annie.

"Okay. You look at that one, and I'll look at the one about castles," said Annie.

"No, we'd better not," said Jack. "We don't know who these books belong to."

But even as he said this, Jack was opening the dinosaur book to the place where the bookmark was. He couldn't help himself.

Jack turned to a picture of an ancient flying reptile. He recognized it as a Pteranodon. He touched the huge bat-like wings in the picture.

"Wow," whispered Jack. "I wish we could

go to the time of Pteranodons."

Jack studied the picture of the odd-looking creature soaring through the sky.

"Ahhh!" screamed Annie.

"What?" said Jack.

"A monster!" Annie cried. She pointed out the tree house window.

"Stop pretending, Annie," said Jack.

"No, really!" said Annie.

Jack looked out the window.

A giant creature was gliding above the treetops! It had a long, weird crest on the back of its head, a skinny beak, and huge bat-like wings!

It was a real live Pteranodon!

The creature swooped through the sky. It looked like a glider plane! It was coming straight toward the tree house!

"Get down!" cried Annie.

Jack and Annie crouched on the floor.

The wind started to blow.

The tree house started to spin.

It spun faster and faster.

Then everything was still.

Absolutely still.

CHAPTER THREE

WHERE IS HERE?

Jack opened his eyes. Sunlight slanted through the window.

The tree house was still high up in a tree.

But it wasn't the *same* tree.

"Where are we?" said Annie. She and Jack looked out the window.

The Pteranodon was soaring through the sky. The ground was covered with ferns and tall grass. There was a winding stream, a sloping hill, and volcanoes in the distance.

"I—I don't know where we are," said Jack.

The Pteranodon glided down to the base of the tree. It landed on the ground and stood very still.

"So what just happened to us?" said Annie.

"Well . . . ," said Jack. "I was looking at the picture in the book—"

"And you said, 'Wow, I wish we could go to the time of Pteranodons,' " said Annie.

"Yeah. And then we saw a Pteranodon in the Frog Creek woods," said Jack.

"Yeah. And then the wind got loud. And the tree house started spinning," said Annie.

"And we landed here," said Jack.

"And we landed here," said Annie.

"So that means . . . ," said Jack.

"So that means . . . what?" said Annie.

"I don't know," said Jack. He shook his head. "None of this can be real."

Annie looked out the window again. "But *he*'s real," she said. "He's *very* real."

Jack looked out the window with her again. The Pteranodon was standing at the base of the tree like a guard. His giant wings were spread out on either side of him.

"Hi!" Annie shouted.

"Shhh!" said Jack. "We're not supposed to be here."

"But where is *here*?" said Annie.

"I don't know," said Jack.

"Hi! Who are you?" Annie called to the Pteranodon.

The creature just looked up at her.

"Are you nuts? He can't talk," said Jack. "But maybe the book can tell us."

Jack looked down at the book. He read the words under the picture:

This flying reptile lived in the Cretaceous Period. It vanished 65 million years ago with the dinosaurs.

"That's impossible!" said Jack. "We can't have gone to a time sixty-five million years ago!"

"Jack," said Annie. "He's nice."

"Nice?" said Jack.

"Yeah, I can tell," said Annie. "Let's go down to him."

"Go down?" said Jack.

Annie started down the rope ladder.

"Hey, come back," said Jack.

But Annie kept going.

"Annie, wait!" Jack called.

Annie dropped to the ground. She stepped boldly up to the ancient creature.

CHAPTER FOUR

HENRY

Jack gasped as Annie reached out her hand toward the Pteranodon.

Oh, no, he thought. Annie was always trying to make friends with animals, but this was going too far.

"Don't get too close to him, Annie!" Jack shouted.

Annie touched the Pteranodon's crest. She stroked his neck. She was talking to him.

What in the world is she saying? Jack wondered.

He took a deep breath. Okay. He would go down, too. It would be good to examine a Pteranodon. He could take notes like a scientist.

Jack started down the rope ladder. When he reached the ground, he was only a few feet away from the creature.

The Pteranodon stared at Jack. His eyes were bright and alert.

"He's soft, Jack," said Annie. "He feels like Henry."

Jack snorted. "He's no dog, Annie."

"Feel him, Jack," said Annie.

Jack didn't move.

"Don't think, Jack. Just do it," Annie said.

Jack stepped forward. He reached out very cautiously. He brushed his hand down the creature's neck.

Interesting, Jack thought. A thin layer of

fuzz covered the Pteranodon's skin.

"Soft, huh?" said Annie.

Jack reached into his backpack and pulled out a pencil and a notebook. He wrote:

fuzzy skin

"What are you doing?" asked Annie.

"Taking notes," said Jack. "We're probably the first people in the whole world to ever see a real live Pteranodon."

Jack looked at the Pteranodon again. The bony crest on top of his head was longer than Jack's arm.

"I wonder how smart he is," Jack said.

"*Very* smart," said Annie.

"Don't count on it," said Jack. "His brain's probably no bigger than a bean."

"No, he's very smart. I can feel it," said Annie. "I'm going to call him Henry."

Jack wrote in his notebook:

small brain?

Jack looked at the creature again. "Maybe he's a mutant," he said.

The Pteranodon tilted his head.

Annie laughed. "He's not a mutant, Jack."

"Well, what's he doing here then? Where is this place?" said Jack.

Annie leaned close to the Pteranodon. "Do you know where we are, Henry?" she asked softly.

The creature fixed his eyes on Annie. His long jaws were opening and closing like a giant pair of scissors.

"Are you trying to talk to me, Henry?" asked Annie.

"Forget it, Annie." Jack wrote in his notebook:

mouth like scissors

"Did we come to a time long ago, Henry?"

asked Annie. "Is this a place from long ago?"

Suddenly Annie gasped. "Jack!"

Jack looked up.

Annie was pointing toward the hill. On top stood a huge dinosaur!

CHAPTER FIVE

GOLD IN THE GRASS

"Go! *Go!*" said Jack. He threw his notebook into his pack. He pushed Annie toward the rope ladder.

"Bye, Henry!" she said.

"Go!" said Jack. He gave Annie another push.

"Quit it!" she said. But she started up the ladder. Jack scrambled after her.

Jack and Annie tumbled into the tree house. They were panting as they looked out the window at the dinosaur. It was standing on the hilltop, eating flowers off a tree.

"Oh, man," whispered Jack. "We *are* in a time long ago!"

The dinosaur looked like a huge rhinoceros with three horns instead of one. It had two long horns above its eyes, and another one grew out from its nose. It had a big shield-like thing behind its head.

"Triceratops!" said Jack.

"Does he eat people?" whispered Annie.

"I'll look it up." Jack grabbed the dinosaur book. He flipped through the pages.

"There!" said Jack, pointing to a picture of a Triceratops. He read the caption:

> The Triceratops lived in the late
> Cretaceous Period. This plant-
> eating dinosaur weighed over
> 12,000 pounds.

Jack slammed the book shut. "Just plants. No meat."

"Good!" said Annie. "Let's go see him up close."

"Are you crazy?" said Jack.

"Don't you want to take notes about him?" asked Annie. "We're probably the first people in the whole world to ever see a real live Triceratops."

Jack sighed. Annie was right.

"Okay, let's go," he said.

Jack shoved the dinosaur book into his pack. He slung his pack over his shoulder. Annie started down the ladder, and Jack followed her.

"Just promise you won't pet him," Jack called down to Annie.

"I promise," said Annie.

"Promise you won't kiss him," said Jack.

"I promise," said Annie.

"Promise you won't talk to him."

"I promise," said Annie.

"Promise you won't—"

"Don't worry!" said Annie.

Annie and Jack stepped off the ladder. The Pteranodon gave them a friendly look.

Annie blew him a kiss. "Be back soon, Henry!" she called.

"Shhh!" said Jack. And he led the way slowly and carefully through the ferns.

When Jack and Annie reached the bottom of the hill, they knelt behind a bush. Annie started to speak, but Jack quickly put his finger to his lips. Then he and Annie peeked out at the Triceratops.

The dinosaur was bigger than a truck. He was eating the flowers off a magnolia tree.

Jack slipped his notebook out of his pack. He wrote:

eats flowers

Annie nudged him.

Jack ignored her. He studied the Triceratops again. He wrote:

eats slowly

Annie nudged him harder.

Jack looked at her.

Annie pointed to herself. She walked her fingers through the air. She pointed to the dinosaur. She smiled.

Is she teasing? Jack wondered.

Annie waved at Jack.

Jack started to grab her.

She laughed and jumped away. She fell into the grass in full view of the Triceratops!

"Get back!" whispered Jack.

Too late. The big dinosaur had spotted Annie. He gazed down at her from the hilltop. Half of a magnolia flower was sticking out of his mouth.

"Oops," said Annie.

"Get back!" Jack said again.

"He looks nice, Jack," Annie said.

"Nice? Watch out for his horns, Annie!" said Jack.

The Triceratops gazed calmly down at Annie. Then he turned and loped down the side of the hill.

"Bye!" said Annie. She turned back to Jack. "See?"

Jack grunted. But he wrote in his notebook:

nice

"Come on. Let's look around some more," said Annie.

As Jack started after Annie, he saw something glittering in the tall grass.

Jack reached down and picked it up. It was a gold medallion.

A letter was engraved on the medallion: a fancy *M*.

"Oh, man. Someone was here before us!" Jack said softly.

CHAPTER SIX

DINOSAUR VALLEY

"Annie, look at this!" Jack called. "Look what I found!"

Annie had gone up to the hilltop. She was picking a flower from the magnolia tree.

"Annie, look! A medallion!" shouted Jack.

But Annie wasn't paying attention to Jack. She was staring at something on the other side of the hill.

"Oh, wow!" she said. Clutching her magnolia flower, she took off down the hill.

"Annie, come back!" Jack shouted.

But Annie had disappeared.

"Oh, brother," Jack muttered. He stuffed the gold medallion into his jeans pocket.

Then Jack heard Annie shriek.

"Annie?" he said.

Jack heard another sound as well—a deep, bellowing sound, like a tuba.

"Jack! Come here, quick!" Annie called.

Jack raced up the hill. When he got to the top, he gasped.

The valley below was filled with nests— big nests made out of mud. The nests were filled with tiny dinosaurs!

Annie was crouching next to one of the nests. Towering over her was a gigantic duck-billed dinosaur!

"Don't panic. Don't move," said Jack. He stepped slowly down the hill toward Annie.

The huge dinosaur was waving her arms and making her tuba sound.

Jack stopped. He didn't want to get too close.

He knelt on the ground. "Okay. Move toward me. Slowly," he said.

Annie started to stand up.

"Don't stand! Crawl," said Jack.

Clutching her flower, Annie crawled toward Jack.

Still bellowing, the duck-billed dinosaur followed her.

Annie froze.

"Keep going," Jack said.

Annie started crawling again.

Jack inched farther down the hill, until he was just an arm's distance from Annie. He reached out and grabbed her hand. He pulled Annie toward him.

"Stay down," Jack said. He crouched next to her. "Bow your head. Pretend to chew."

"Chew?" said Annie.

"Yes," said Jack. "I read that's what you

do if a mean dog comes at you."

"She's no dog, Jack," said Annie.

"Just chew," said Jack.

Jack and Annie both bowed their heads and pretended to chew. Soon the dinosaur grew quiet.

Jack looked up. "I don't think she's mad anymore," he said.

"You saved me," said Annie. "Thanks."

"You have to use your brain, Annie," said Jack. "You can't just go running to a nest of babies. There's always a mother nearby."

Annie stood up.

"Annie, don't!" said Jack.

Too late.

Annie held out her magnolia flower to the dinosaur.

"I'm sorry I made you worry about your babies," she said.

The dinosaur moved closer to Annie.

She grabbed the flower from her hand. She reached for another.

"No more," said Annie.

The dinosaur let out a sad tuba sound.

"But there are more flowers up there," Annie said. She pointed to the top of the hill. "I'll get you some."

Annie hurried up the hill.

The dinosaur waddled after her.

Jack quickly looked at the dinosaur babies. Some were crawling out of their nests.

Where are the other mothers? Jack wondered.

Jack took out the dinosaur book. He flipped through the pages. He found a picture of some duck-billed dinosaurs. He read the caption:

The Anatosauruses lived in colonies. While a few mothers babysat the nests, others looked for food.

So there were probably more mothers close by, looking for food.

"Hey, Jack!" Annie called.

Jack looked up. Annie was at the top of the hill, feeding magnolia flowers to the giant Anatosaurus!

"Guess what?" Annie said. "She's nice, too."

Suddenly the Anatosaurus made her terrible tuba sound. Annie crouched down and started to chew.

The dinosaur charged down the hill. She seemed afraid of something.

Jack put the book on top of his pack. He hurried to Annie.

"I wonder why she ran away," said Annie. "We were starting to be friends."

Jack looked around. What he saw in the distance almost made him faint!

An enormous monster was coming across the plain.

The monster was walking on two strong legs. It was swinging a long, thick tail and dangling two tiny arms.

It had a huge head—and its jaws were wide open.

Even from far away Jack could see its long, gleaming teeth.

"Tyrannosaurus rex!" whispered Jack.

CHAPTER SEVEN

READY, SET, GO!

"Run, Annie! Run!" cried Jack. "Run to the tree house!"

Jack and Annie dashed down the hill together. They ran through the tall grass and ferns and past the Pteranodon.

They scrambled up the rope ladder and tumbled into the tree house.

Annie leaped to the window.

"It's going away!" she said, panting.

Jack pushed his glasses into place. He looked out the window with Annie.

The Tyrannosaurus was wandering off.

But then the monster stopped and turned around.

"Duck!" said Jack.

The two of them ducked their heads.

After a long moment, they peeked out the window again.

"Coast clear," said Jack.

"Yay," whispered Annie.

"We have to get out of here," said Jack.

"You made a wish before," said Annie.

"Right," said Jack. He took a deep breath. "I wish we could go back to Frog Creek!"

Nothing happened.

"I said I wish—" started Jack.

"Wait," said Annie. "You were looking at a picture in the dinosaur book. Remember?"

"Oh, no, I left the book and my pack on the hill!" said Jack. "I have to go back!"

"Forget it," said Annie.

"I can't," said Jack. "The book doesn't belong to us. Plus my notebook with all my notes is in my pack. And my—"

"Okay, okay!" said Annie.

"I'll hurry!" said Jack. He climbed quickly down the ladder and leaped to the ground.

Jack raced past the Pteranodon, through the ferns, through the tall grass, and up the hill.

He looked down.

His pack was lying on the ground. On top of it was the dinosaur book.

But now the valley below was filled with Anatosauruses. They were all standing guard around the nests.

Where had they been? Did fear of the Tyrannosaurus send them home?

Jack took a deep breath. *Ready! Set! Go!* he thought.

He charged down the hill. He ran to his backpack. He scooped it up. He grabbed the dinosaur book.

Jack heard a terrible tuba sound! Then another, and another! All the Anatosauruses were bellowing at him!

Jack took off.

He raced up to the hilltop.

He started down the hill.

He stopped.

The Tyrannosaurus rex was back! It was standing between Jack and the tree house!

thod. The monster still didn't seem to notice them.

CHAPTER EIGHT

A GIANT SHADOW

Jack jumped behind the magnolia tree.

His heart was beating so fast he could hardly think.

He peeked out at the giant monster. The horrible-looking creature was opening and closing its huge jaws. Its teeth were as big as steak knives.

Don't panic, thought Jack. *Think*.

He peered down at the valley.

Good. The duck-billed dinosaurs were sticking close to their nests.

Jack looked back at the Tyrannosaurus.

Good. The monster still didn't seem to know he was there.

Don't panic. Think. Think. Maybe there's information in the book.

Jack opened the dinosaur book. He found Tyrannosaurus rex. He read:

Tyrannosaurus rex was one of the largest meat-eating land animals of all time. If it were alive today, it could eat a human in one bite.

Great, thought Jack. The book was no help at all.

Jack tried to think clearly. He couldn't hide on the other side of the hill. The Anatosauruses might stampede.

He couldn't run to the tree house. The

Tyrannosaurus might run faster.

Maybe he should just wait for the monster to leave.

Jack peeked around the tree.

The Tyrannosaurus had wandered *closer* to the hill.

Something caught Jack's eye. Annie was coming down the rope ladder!

Is she nuts? What is she doing? Jack wondered.

Jack watched Annie hop off the ladder.

Annie hurried over to the Pteranodon. She was talking to him. She was flapping her arms. She pointed at Jack, at the sky, at the tree house.

She is *nuts!* Jack thought.

"Go! Go back up in the tree!" Jack whispered. "Go!"

Jack heard a roar.

The Tyrannosaurus rex was looking in his direction.

Jack hit the ground.

The Tyrannosaurus rex was coming toward the hill.

Jack felt the ground shaking.

What should I do? Jack wondered. *Should I run? Crawl back into Dinosaur Valley? Climb the magnolia tree?*

Suddenly a giant shadow covered Jack. He looked up.

The Pteranodon was gliding overhead. The giant creature sailed toward the top of the hill.

He was heading toward Jack.

CHAPTER NINE

THE AMAZING RIDE

The Pteranodon coasted down to the ground.

He stared at Jack with his bright, alert eyes.

What was Jack supposed to do? Climb on?
But I'm too heavy, thought Jack.

Jack looked at the Tyrannosaurus. It was starting up the hill. Its giant teeth were flashing in the sunlight.

Okay, thought Jack. *Don't think! Just do it!*

Jack put his book in his pack. Then he climbed onto the Pteranodon's back. He held on tightly.

The creature moved forward. He spread his wings—and lifted off the ground!

Jack nearly fell off as they teetered this way and that.

The Pteranodon steadied himself and rose into the sky.

Jack looked down. The Tyrannosaurus was staring up at him and chomping the air.

The Pteranodon glided away.

He sailed over the hilltop and over the valley.

He circled above all the duck-billed dinosaurs and all the nests filled with babies.

Then the Pteranodon soared out over the plain—over the Triceratops, who was grazing in the high grass.

Jack felt like a bird. The wind was rushing through his hair. The air smelled sweet and fresh.

Jack whooped and laughed. He couldn't believe it! He was riding on the back of an ancient flying reptile!

The Pteranodon sailed over the stream and over the ferns and bushes. Then he carried Jack down to the base of the oak tree.

When they came to a stop, Jack slid off the creature's back and landed on the ground.

The Pteranodon took off again and glided into the sky.

"Bye, Henry!" called Jack.

"Jack! Are you okay?" Annie shouted from the tree house.

Jack pushed his glasses into place. He kept staring at the Pteranodon.

"Jack!" Annie called.

Jack looked up at Annie. He smiled.

"Thanks for saving my life," he said. "That was really fun."

"Thank Henry, not me!" said Annie. "Come on! Climb up!"

Jack tried to stand. His legs were wobbly. He felt a bit dizzy.

"Hurry!" shouted Annie. "It's coming!"

Jack looked around. The Tyrannosaurus

was heading straight toward him! Jack bolted to the ladder. He started climbing.

"Hurry! Hurry!" screamed Annie.

Jack reached the top and scrambled into the tree house.

"It's coming toward the tree!" Annie cried.

The dinosaur slammed against the oak tree. The tree house shook like a leaf in the wind.

Jack and Annie tumbled into the books.

"Make a wish to go home!" cried Annie.

"We need the book! The Pennsylvania book!" said Jack. "Where is it?"

They both searched madly around the tree house.

"Found it!" said Jack.

He grabbed the book and flipped through the pages. He found the photograph of the Frog Creek woods.

Jack pointed to the picture in the book.

"I wish we could go home!" he shouted.

The wind began to blow.

Jack closed his eyes. He held on tightly to Annie.

The tree house started to spin.

It spun faster and faster.

Then everything was still.

Absolutely still.

CHAPTER TEN

HOME BEFORE DARK

Jack heard a bird singing.

He opened his eyes. He was still pointing at the picture of the Frog Creek woods.

He peeked out the tree house window. Outside he saw the exact same view as the picture in the book.

"We're home," whispered Annie.

The woods were lit with a golden late-afternoon light. The sun was about to set.

No time had passed since they'd left Frog Creek.

"Ja-ack! An-nie!" a voice called from the
distance.

"That's Mom," said Annie.

Jack saw their mother far away. She was
standing in front of their house. She looked tiny.

"An-nie! Ja-ack!" she called.

Annie stuck her head out the window and shouted, "Coming!"

Jack still felt dazed. He just stared at Annie.

"What happened to us?" he said.

"We took a trip in a magic tree house," said Annie simply.

"But it's the same time as when we left," said Jack.

Annie shrugged.

"How did it take us so far away?" said Jack. "And so long ago?"

"You looked at a picture in a book and said you wished we could go there," said Annie. "And the magic tree house took us there."

"But *how*?" said Jack. "And who built this magic tree house? Who put all these books here?"

"A magic person, I guess," said Annie.

"Oh, look," said Jack. "I almost forgot about this."

Jack reached into his pocket and pulled out the gold medallion. "Someone lost this back there," he said, "in dinosaur land. Look, there's a letter *M* on it."

Annie's eyes got round. "You think *M* stands for *magic person*?" she asked.

"I don't know," said Jack. "I just know someone went to that place before us."

"Ja-ack! An-nie!" their mom called again.

"Coming!" Annie shouted again.

Jack put the gold medallion back in his pocket. He pulled the dinosaur book out of his pack and put it back with all the other books.

Then he and Annie took one last look around the tree house.

"Good-bye, house," whispered Annie.

Jack slung his backpack over his shoulders.

Annie started down the rope ladder. Jack followed.

Seconds later they hopped onto the ground and started walking out of the woods.

"No one's going to believe our story," said Jack.

"So let's not tell anyone," said Annie.

"Dad won't believe it," said Jack.

"He'll say it was a dream," said Annie.

"Mom won't believe it," said Jack.

"She'll say it was pretend."

"My teacher won't believe it," said Jack.

"She'll say you're nuts," said Annie.

"We'd better not tell anyone," said Jack.

"I already said that," said Annie.

Jack sighed. "I think I'm starting not to believe it myself," he said.

They left the woods and started up the road toward their house.

As they walked past all the houses on their street, the trip to dinosaur time *did* seem more and more like a dream.

Only *this* world and *this* time seemed real.

Jack reached into his pocket. He clasped the gold medallion.

He felt the engraving of the letter *M*. It made his fingers tingle.

Jack laughed. Suddenly he felt very happy.

He couldn't explain what had happened today. But he knew for sure that their trip in the magic tree house had been real.

Absolutely real.

"Tomorrow," Jack said softly, "we'll go back to the woods."

"Of course," said Annie.

"And we'll climb up to the tree house," said Jack.

"Of course," said Annie.

"And we'll see what happens next," said Jack.

"Of course," said Annie. "Race you!"

And they took off together, running for home.

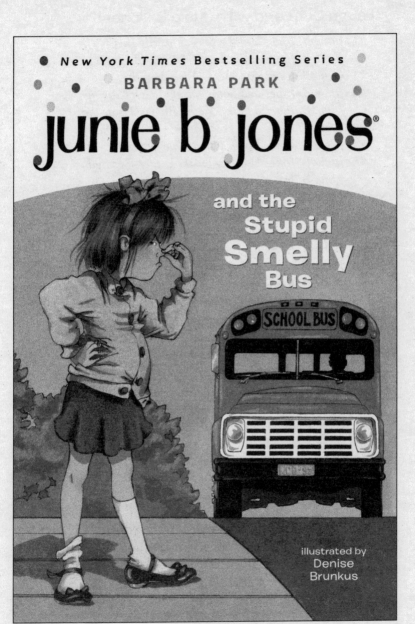

BARBARA PARK

junie b jones®

and the
Stupid
Smelly
Bus

illustrated by
Denise
Brunkus

Laugh Out Loud with Junie B. Jones!

junie b. jones®
and the
Stupid Smelly Bus

by BARBARA PARK

illustrated by
Denise Brunkus

A STEPPING STONE BOOK™

Random House New York

Contents

1
Meeting Mrs.

My name is Junie B. Jones. The B stands for Beatrice. Except I don't like Beatrice. I just like B and that's all.

I'm almost six years old.

Almost six is when you get to go to kindergarten. Kindergarten is where you go to meet new friends and not watch TV.

My kindergarten is the afternoon kind.

Today was my first day of school. I'd been to my room before, though. Last week Mother took me there to meet my teacher.

It was called Meet the Teacher Day. My teacher was decorating the bulletin board with the letters of the alphabet.

"I already know all of those letters," I said. "I can sing them. Except I don't feel like it right now."

My teacher shook my hand. Only our hands didn't fit together that good.

Her name was Mrs.—I can't remember the rest of it. Mrs. said I looked cute.

"I know it," I said. "That's because I have on my new shoes."

I held my foot way high in the air.

"See how shiny they are? Before I put them on, I licked them.

"And guess what else?" I said. "This is my bestest hat. Grampa Miller bought it for me. See the devil horns sticking out the sides?"

Mrs. laughed. Except I don't know why. Devil horns are supposed to be scary.

Then we walked around the room and she showed me where stuff was. Like the easels where we get to paint. And the shelves where the books are. And the tables where we sit and don't watch TV.

One of the tables in the front of the room had a red chair. "I would like to sit here, I think," I told her.

But Mrs. said, "We'll have to wait and see, Junie."

"B!" I said. "Call me Junie *B*.!"

I hollered the B part real loud. So she wouldn't forget it.

People are *always* forgetting my B.

Mother rolled her eyes and looked at the ceiling. I looked up there, too. But I didn't see anything.

"Are you going to ride the bus, Junie B.?" Mrs. asked me.

I made my shoulders go up and down. "I don't know. Where's it goin' to?"

My mother nodded her head and said, "Yes, she'll be riding the bus."

That made me feel scary inside. 'Cause I never rided on a bus before.

"Yeah, only where's it goin' to?" I asked again.

Mrs. sat on her desk. Then she and my mother talked more about the bus.

I tapped on Mrs.

"Guess what? I still don't know where it's goin' to."

Mrs. smiled and said the bus driver's name was Mr. Woo.

"Mr. Woo," said Mother. "That's an easy name for Junie B. to remember."

I covered my ears and stamped my foot. "YEAH, ONLY WHERE'S THE STUPID SMELLY BUS GOIN' TO?"

Mother and Mrs. frowned.

Frowning is when your eyebrows look grumpy.

"Watch yourself, missy," said Mother.

Missy's my name when I'm in trouble.

I looked down at my shoes. They didn't look as shiny as they did before.

Just then another mother and a boy came in. And Mrs. went off to talk to them instead of me. I don't know why, though. The boy was hiding behind his mother and acting very babyish. I can beat that boy up, I think.

After that, my mother sat me down and explained about the bus. She said it's yellow. And it's called a school bus. And it stops at the end of my street.

Then I get on it. And sit down. And it takes me to school.

"And then your teacher will meet you in

the parking lot," said Mother. "Okay, Junie B.? Won't that be fun?"

I nodded the word *yes*.

But inside my head I said the word *no*.

2
Feeling Squeezy

I stayed scared about the bus for a whole week. And last night when my mother tucked me into bed, I still felt sickish about it.

"Guess what?" I said. "I don't think I want to ride that school bus to kindergarten tomorrow."

Then my mother rumpled my hair. "Oh, sure you do," she said.

"Oh, sure I don't," I said back.

Then Mother kissed me and said, "It'll be fun. You'll see. Just don't worry."

I did, though. I worried very much. And I didn't sleep so good, either.

And this morning I felt very droopy when I got up. And my stomach was squeezy. And I couldn't eat my cereal.

And so I watched TV until Mother said it was time to get ready to go.

Then I put on my skirt that looks like velvet. And my new fuzzy pink sweater. And I ate half a tuna sandwich for lunch.

After that, Mother and I walked to the corner to wait for the bus.

And guess what? There was another mother and little girl there, too. The little girl had curly black hair—which is my favorite kind of head.

I didn't say hello to her, though. 'Cause she was from a different street, that's why.

Then finally this big yellow bus came around the corner. And the brakes screeched very loud. And I had to cover my ears.

Then the door opened.

And the bus driver said, "Hi! I'm Mr. Woo. Hop on!"

Except I didn't hop on. 'Cause my legs didn't want to.

"I don't think I want to ride this bus to kindergarten," I told Mother again.

Then she gave me a little push. "Go on, Junie B.," she said. "Mr. Woo is waiting for you. Be a big girl and get on."

I looked up at the windows. The little girl with the curly black hair was already in the bus. She looked very big sitting up there. And kind of happy.

"Look how big *that* little girl is acting, Junie B.," said Mother. "Why don't you sit right next to her? It'll be fun. I promise."

And so I got on the bus.

And guess what?

It wasn't fun.

3

The Stupid Smelly Bus

The bus wasn't like my daddy's car at all. It was very big inside. And the seats didn't have any cloth on them.

The little curly girl was sitting near the front. And so I tapped on her.

"Guess what?" I said. "Mother said for me to sit here."

"No!" she said. "I'm saving this seat for my best friend, Mary Ruth Marble!"

Then she put her little white purse on the place where I was going to sit.

And so I made a face at her.

"Hurry up and find a seat, young lady," said Mr. Woo.

And so I quick sat down across from the curly mean girl. And Mr. Woo shut the door.

It wasn't a regular kind of door, though. It folded in half. And when it closed, it made a whishy sound.

I don't like that kind of door. If it closes on you by accident, it will cut you in half, and you will make a squishy sound.

The bus made a big roar. Then a big puff of black smelly smoke came out the back end of it. It's called bus breath, I think.

Mr. Woo drove for a while. Then the brakes made that loud, screechy noise again. I covered my ears so it couldn't get inside my head. 'Cause if loud, screechy noises get inside your head, you have to take an aspirin. I saw that on a TV commercial.

Then the bus door opened again. And a dad and a boy with a grouchy face got on.

The dad smiled. Then he plopped the grouchy boy right next to me.

"This is Jim," he said. "I'm afraid Jim isn't too happy this afternoon."

The dad kissed the boy good-bye. But the boy wiped it off his cheek.

Jim had on a backpack. It was blue.

I love backpacks. I wish I had one of my very own. One time I found a red one in a trash can. But it had a little bit of gushy on it, and Mother said no.

Jim's backpack had lots of zippers. I touched each one of them.

"One . . . two . . . three . . . four," I counted.

Then I unzipped one.

"HEY! DON'T!" yelled Jim.

He zipped it right up again. Then he moved to the seat in front of me.

I hate that Jim.

After that, the bus kept stopping and starting. And lots of kids kept getting on. Loud kids. And some of them were the kind who look like meanies.

Then the bus began getting very noisy and hot inside. And the sun kept shining down on me and my fuzzy hot sweater.

And here's another hot thing. I couldn't roll down my window because it didn't have a handle. And so I just kept on getting hotter and hotter.

And it smelled in the bus, too. The bus smelled like an egg salad sandwich.

"I want to get off of here," I said right

out loud. But nobody heard me. "I hate it in this stupid smelly bus."

Then my eyes got a little bit wet. I wasn't crying, though. 'Cause I'm not a baby, that's why.

After that, my nose started running. Only the bus didn't have a glove compartment. Which is where you keep the travel tissues, of course. And so I had to wipe my nose on my fuzzy pink sweater sleeve.

Then I stayed on the bus for about an hour or three. Until finally I saw a flagpole and a playground.

That meant we were at kindergarten!

Then Mr. Woo drove the bus into the parking lot and stopped.

I jumped up very fast. 'Cause all I wanted to do was get off that stupid smelly thing!

Only guess what? That Jim pushed right

in front of me. And the curly mean girl did, too. And then people started squishing me real tight. And so I pushed them away. And they pushed me right back.

That's when I fell down! And a big foot stepped on my skirt that looks like velvet.

"STOP IT!" I yelled.

Then Mr. Woo hollered, "HEY, HEY, HEY!"

And he picked me up. And helped me off the bus.

Mrs. was waiting for me just like my mother said.

"Hi! I'm glad to see you!" she called.

Then I ran over to her. And I showed her the big footprint on my skirt that looks like velvet.

"Yeah, only look what happened. I got stepped on and so now I'm soiled."

Mrs. brushed it. "Don't worry, Junie," she said. "It'll come off."

After that I just folded my arms and made a frown.

'Cause guess what?

She forgot my B again.

4

Me and Lucille
and Some Other Kids

Some of the other bus kids turned out to be in my class, too.

One of them was that Jim.

That Jim I hate.

Mrs. made us line up. Then we followed her to our room. Its name is Room Nine.

There were other kids waiting by the door. When Mrs. unlocked it, everyone squeezed in all at once.

That Jim stepped on my new shoe. He made a scratch mark on my shiny toe. The kind of scratch that licking won't fix.

"HEY! WATCH IT, YOU DUMB JIM!" I hollered at him.

Mrs. bent down next to me. "Let's try to use our quiet voice while we're in school," she said.

I nodded nicely. "I hate that Jim," I said in my quiet voice.

After that, Mrs. clapped her hands together very loud.

"I want everyone to find a chair and sit down as fast as you can," she said.

That's when I ran to the table with the red chair. Only guess what? There was already someone sitting there! A girl with little red fingernails.

And so I tapped on her and said, "I would like to sit there, I think."

"No," she said. "*I* am."

"Yeah, only I already picked that chair out," I told her. "Ask my mother if you don't believe me."

But the girl just shook her head no.

And then Mrs. clapped her loud hands again and said, "Please find a seat!"

And so then I had to quick sit down in a stupid yellow chair.

The same stupid color as the stupid yellow bus.

After that, Mrs. walked to a big closet in the back of the room. It's called the supply closet. She got out boxes of new pointy crayons and some white circles. Then she passed them out. And we had to print our names on the circles and pin them to our fronts.

It was our first work.

"If you need help spelling your name, raise your hand," said Mrs.

I raised my hand.

"I don't need help," I told her. "Grandma Miller says I print beautifully."

I used red. But then a mistake happened. I made my **JUNIE** too big and there wasn't any room left for my **B**. And so I had to squish it very teeny at the bottom.

"I HATE THIS STUPID DUMB CIRCLE!" I hollered.

Mrs. made the *shhh* sound and gave me a new one.

"Thank you," I said nicely. "Grandma Miller says I print beautifully."

The girl with the little red fingernails was faster than me. She showed me her circle and pointed to her letters.

"L-U-C-I-L-L-E. That spells *Lucille*," she said.

"I like that name of Lucille," I said. "'Cause guess why? Seals are my favorite animals. That's why."

Then Mrs. passed out drawing paper. And we drew pictures of our family.

Mrs. put a happy-face sticker on mine.

It was very good. Except I made my father too teeny. And Mother's hair looked like sticks.

After that, Mrs. took our class on a walk around the school. Everyone had to find a buddy to walk with.

My buddy was Lucille. We held hands.

The boy I can beat up was right in front of us. His buddy was that Jim.

That Jim I hate.

The first place we walked to is called the Media Center. My mother calls it a library. It's where the books are. And guess what?

Books are my favorite things in the whole world!

"HEY! THERE'S A JILLION OF THEM IN HERE!" I hollered, feeling very excited. "I THINK I LOVE THIS PLACE!"

The librarian bent down next to me. She said to use my quiet voice.

"YEAH, ONLY GUESS WHAT? RIGHT NOW I JUST LIKE THE KIND OF BOOKS WITH PICTURES. BUT MOTHER SAYS WHEN I GET BIG, I'M GOING TO LIKE THE KIND WITH JUST WORDS. AND ALSO, STEWED TOMATOES."

The boy I can beat up said, "Shhh."

I made a fist at him.

Then he turned around.

After that, we went to the cafeteria. The cafeteria is where kids eat lunch. Except not when you're in kindergarten.

"Ummm!" I said. "It smells yummy in here! Just like pasketti and meatballs!"

Then that Jim turned around and held his nose.

"P.U. . . . I smell you," he said.

Lucille laughed very hard.

And so I stopped holding her hand.

The next place we went to was the nurse's office.

It's very cute in that place. There are two little beds where you get to lie down. And two little blankets that are the color of plaid.

Our nurse doesn't look like a nurse. She doesn't wear white clothes and white shoes.

Our nurse is just a regular color.

Lucille raised her hand. "My brother said that last year he came here. And you let him take off his shoes. And he got a drink of water in just his socks!"

That Jim turned around again.

"P.U. . . . I smell your feet," he said to Lucille.

This time Lucille stuck out her tongue at him.

After that, we held hands again.

5
Principal

After we left the nurse, we went to the main office. That's where the boss of the school lives. His name is Principal.

Principal is a baldy.

He talked to us.

Then Lucille raised her hand. "My brother said that last year he had to come down here. And you yelled at him. And now he's not allowed to beat up kids at recess anymore."

Principal kind of laughed. Then he held the door for us to leave.

After that, we walked to the water fountain. And Mrs. let us get a drink. I didn't get a long one, though. 'Cause kids kept tapping on me.

"Hurry up, girl," they said.

"Yeah, only guess what? That's not even my name," I told them.

"Her name is Junie Bumblebee," said Lucille.

Then she laughed. But I didn't think it was a very funny joke.

After that, Mrs. showed us where the bathrooms were.

There's two kinds of bathrooms in our school. A boys' kind. And a girls' kind. I can't go in the boys' kind, though. 'Cause no girls allowed, that's why.

I tried to peek my head in there. But Mrs. snapped her fingers at me.

The only boy who got to go into the bathroom was the boy I can beat up. He was jiggling around very much.

Then he started running all over the place. And he was holding the front of his pants.

"William!" said Mrs. "Are you having an emergency?"

Then William yelled, "YES!" And he ran right in there.

The rest of us walked back to our room.

I touched Lucille's fingernails. She said that her fingernail polish is named Very Very Berry.

"I would like to have my fingernails red, too," I said. "But I'm only allowed to have the kind of polish that makes them look shiny. Its name is Clear. Clear is the color of spit."

"I hate Clear," said Lucille.

"Me too," I told her. "And also I hate

yellow—which is the color of the stupid smelly school bus."

Lucille nodded her head. "My brother said when you ride home on the bus, kids pour chocolate milk on your head."

Then all of a sudden my stomach felt very squeezy again. 'Cause I had to ride the bus home, that's why.

"Why did you have to tell me that for, Lucille?" I said kind of grouchy.

After we got back to Room Nine, we did some more work. It was a game to help us learn each other's names.

I learned Lucille. And also a girl named Charlotte. And another girl named Grace. Then I learned a boy named Ham—which we eat at Grandma Miller's.

Pretty soon Mrs. clapped her loud hands together.

"Okay, everyone. Gather up your things.

It's almost time for the bell."

Then I heard a noise in the parking lot. It was screechy brakes. And so I looked out the window. And I saw the school bus.

It was coming to get me!

"Oh no!" I said kind of loud. "Now I'm going to get chocolate milk poured on my head!" Then I chewed on my fingers.

"Get in line! Get in line!" said Mrs. "When we get outside, I want all of my bus students to come with me. The rest of you must go to the crossing guard."

Everyone was lining up. I was the very last one.

Just then the bell rang and Mrs. marched out the door. Then everybody else marched out, too.

Except guess what?

I didn't.

6

A Good Hider

When you're the very last one in line, nobody watches you. That's how come nobody saw me when I ducked behind the teacher's desk and hid.

I'm a good hider.

One time at Grandma Miller's house, I hid under the kitchen sink. Then I made a growly sound and sprung out at her.

I'm not allowed to do that anymore.

Anyway, I stayed scrunched behind the teacher's desk for a while. And then I saw a better place to hide. It was the big supply closet in the back of the room.

And so I ran back there very fast. And I squeezed onto the bottom shelf. I squeezed right on top of the construction paper.

Most of me was comfortable. Except my head was sort of very tight. And my knees were all bended. Like when I do a somersault.

Then I pulled the door mostly closed.

"Don't shut it all the way, though. And I *mean* it," I said right out loud.

I stayed real quiet for lots of minutes. Then I heard noises in the hall. And some feet came running into the room. Big people's feet, I think.

"What happened?" I heard someone ask.

"One of my little girls is lost," said a voice that sounded like Mrs. "Her name is Junie B. Jones. And she didn't get on the bus. So now we've got to go out looking for her."

Then I heard some keys jingle. And the feet went running out again. And then the door shut.

I still didn't come out of the closet, though. When you're a good hider, you can't come out for a very, very long time.

I just stayed there all bended up. And I

told myself a story. Not an out-loud story. I just told it inside my head. It was called "The Little Hiding Girl."

I made it up. And this is how it went:

Once upon a time there was a little hiding girl. She was in a secret spot where nobody could find her. Except her head was very tight. And her brain was squishing out.

But she still couldn't come out of her spot. Or a smelly yellow monster would get her. And also, some meanies with chocolate milk.

The end.

After that, I rested my eyes.

Resting your eyes is what my grampa does when he watches TV after dinner. Then he snores. And Grandma Miller says, "Go to bed, Frank."

It's not the same thing as a nap, though.

'Cause naps are for babies, that's why.

And anyway, I didn't snore. I just did a little drool.

Then finally when my eyes were done resting, they woke up.

And so I came out of the closet and ran right to the window. And guess what? There weren't any cars in the parking lot. And no stupid smelly bus, either!

"Whew! That's a relief," I said.

A relief is when your stomach doesn't feel squeezy anymore.

After that, I went back to the closet. 'Cause while I was hiding, I sniffed the smell of clay, that's why. And clay is my very favorite thing in the whole world!

"Hey! I see it up there!" I said.

The clay was on the middle shelf. I stood on a chair to get it.

It was blue and stiff. And so I had to roll it on the floor to make it soft and warm. Then I rolled it into a blue orange. It was very beautiful. Except it had some dirt and hair on it.

After I was done, I went to the front of the room and sat down in my teacher's big chair. I like teachers' desks very much. The drawers are so big I could fit in one, I think.

I opened up the top one. There were happy-face stickers. And rubber bands. And also, gold stars—which I love a very lot.

I stuck one on my forehead.

Then I found paper clips. And red marking pens. And new pencils with no points. And scissors. And travel tissues. And guess what else?

"Chalk!" I said. "Brand-new chalk that's not even out of its little box yet!"

Then I stood up on my teacher's chair and clapped my hands together very loud.

"I want everyone to find a chair and sit down! Today we are going to learn some alphabet and some reading. And also, I will teach you how to make a blue orange. But first, everyone has to watch me draw stuff."

Then I went to the board and drew with my brand-new chalk. I drew a bean and a carrot and some curly hair.

Then I wrote some **O**'s.

O's are my bestest letter.

After that, I bowed. "Thank you very much," I said. "Now you may all go out for recess . . ."

I smiled.

"Except for not that Jim."

7

Peeky Holes and Spying

After a while, I started to get a little bit thirsty. That's what happens when chalk sprinkles get in your throat.

"I would like a drink of water, I think," I said.

Then I put my hands on my hips. "Yeah, only what if somebody sees you at the water fountain? Then they might call the stupid smelly bus to come get you. And so you better not go."

I stamped my foot. "Yeah, only I *have* to

go! 'Cause there's dumb chalk in my throat!"

Then all of a sudden I got a great idea! I pulled a chair over to the door. And I peeked out the window at the top!

I'm a good peeker.

One time I peeked right into Grampa Miller's mouth when he was sleeping. And I saw that dangly thing that hangs down in the back. I didn't touch it, though. 'Cause I didn't have a little stick or anything, that's why.

Anyway, I didn't see anybody in the hall. And so I opened the door a crack. And I sniffed. 'Cause when you sniff, you can smell if there's people around.

I learned sniffing from my dog, Tickle. Dogs can smell everything. People can mostly just smell big smells. Like stink and flowers and dinner.

"Nope. Don't smell anyone," I said.

Then I ran to the water fountain and I drank for a long time. And nobody tapped on me and said, "Hurry up, girl."

After that, I stood on my tippy-toes. And I tippy-toed to the Media Center. 'Cause I love that place! Remember?

The Media Center is kind of like a fort. The shelves are like walls. And the books are sort of like bricks. And you can move some of them around and make peeky holes.

Peeky holes are what you spy out of.

Then if you see somebody coming, you can make your breath very quiet. And they won't find you.

I spied for a long time. But nobody came. The only people in the Media Center were just me and some fish.

The fish were in a big glass tank. I waved

at them in there. Then I stirred them with a pencil.

I love fish very much. I eat them for dinner with coleslaw.

Just then I saw my most favorite thing in the whole world! Its name is an electric pencil sharpener! And it was sitting right on the librarian's desk!

"Hey!" I said very excited. "I think I know how to work that thing!"

Then I looked in the desk drawer. And guess what? There were lots of brand-new pencils in there!

And so I sharpened them!

It was funner than anything! 'Cause an electric pencil sharpener makes a nice noise. And you can make pencils as teeny as you want. You just keep pushing them into the little hole. And they just keep on getting teenier and teenier.

It doesn't work on crayons, though. I tried a red one. Then the pencil sharpener slowed way down. And then it made a *rrrrr-rrrrr* sound. And after that, it didn't go anymore.

Just then I heard a noise! It was walking feet. And it made me scared inside. 'Cause I didn't want anyone to find me, that's why!

And so I squatted way down and looked through my peeky hole.

Then I saw a man with a trash can! He was singing "Somewhere Over the Rainbow." That's a song I know. It's from my favorite movie, which is called *The Wizard of Odds*.

The man with the can didn't see me. He walked down the hall. Then I heard him go outside. I stayed squatted down for a long time. But he never came back.

"Whew! That was a close one!" I said.

And so then I ran to find a better place to hide.

8

The Dangerous
Nurse's Office

Guess where I ran to? Straight to the nurse's office, of course! 'Cause there's those little plaid blankets to hide under!

There's other neat stuff in there, too. Like a scale to weigh yourself. And a sign with a giant E and other letters.

The nurse uses the sign to test your eyes. She points to the letters. And you have to yell out their names.

You have to yell the E the loudest. That's how come it's so big.

And guess what else I saw in the nurse's office? Band-Aids, that's what! I love those guys!

They were on top of the desk. And so I opened the lid. And I sniffed them.

"Ummm," I said. 'Cause Band-Aids smell just like a brand-new beach ball.

Then I dumped them out. They were the most prettiest Band-Aids I ever saw! They were red and blue and green! And also yellow. Which is the color I hate.

And they were different shapes, too. There were squares and circles. And some were that very long kind—which are called tangles, I think.

I put a green circle on my knee. That's where I fell down on the sidewalk last week. It's mostly all better now. But if I press it very hard with my thumb, I can still make it hurt.

After that, I put a blue tangle on my finger. That's where I got a splinter from the picnic table. Mother pulled it out with tweezers. But there's still some table in there, I think.

Also, I put a red square on my arm. That's where Tickle scratched me. Because I got him all wound up.

Just then I saw the nurse's purple sweater. It was hanging on her chair.

I put it on.

"Now I'm the nurse," I said.

Then I sat down. And I pretended to call the hospital.

"Hello, hospital? It's me, the nurse. I need some more Band-Aids and some aspirins and some cherry cough drops. Only not the kind that make your mouth feel freezy.

"And I need some lollipops for when kids get needles.

"And also I need a little stick or something in case I have to touch that dangly thing that hangs down in your throat."

Then I pretended to call Room Nine.

"Hello, Mrs.? Please send that Jim to my office. I have to give him a shot."

Just then I saw my most favorite thing in the whole world! They were near the door. And their name is crutches!

Crutches are for when you break a leg. Then the doctor puts it in a big white cast with just your piggies sticking out. And you can't walk on it. And so she gives you crutches to swing yourself.

I ran over and picked them up. Then I put them under my arms. Only they were way too long for me. And I didn't swing that good.

And so then I got another idea! I carried them to the nurse's chair. And I climbed up

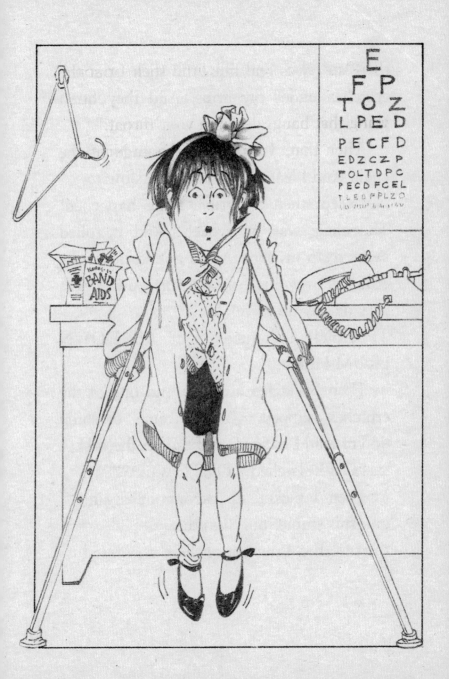

there so I was real tall. And then I put the crutches under my arms. And they fitted just right!

After that, I stood on the edge of the chair. And I leaned forward very slow.

Except then a terrible thing happened! The chair was on wheels. And it rolled away from my feet! And I got stuck on the crutches way high in the air! And I was very dangly up there!

"HEY!" I shouted. "GET ME DOWN FROM HERE!"

Then I wiggled around. And one of the crutches slipped. And I came crashing down! And I banged my head on the desk!

"OW!" I yelled. "OW! OW! OW!"

Then I picked up the phone again. "I quit this stupid job!" I said.

And then I ran out of there very fast.

'Cause the nurse's office is a dangerous place.

And crutches aren't my favorite thing.

9

Zooming Speedy Fast

I like running inside the school.

It's funner than running inside your house. In school you can zoom with your arms out like a jet plane. And you don't knock over the furniture. And also the head doesn't get broken off your mother's bird statue. Which used to be a blue jay, I think.

I zoomed straight to the cafeteria. 'Cause there's a lot of tables to hide under in that place. Only when I tried to open the door, it was all locked up!

And so then I ran to another room across the hall. Only that stupid door was locked, too!

"Hey! Who did all this dumb locking?" I asked.

Then I started jiggling up and down. 'Cause I was having a little bit of a problem, that's why. The kind of problem that's called *personal*.

And it's about going to the potty.

And so all of a sudden I had to run down the hall speedy quick!

Right to the girls' bathroom!

Only guess what? When I got there, that stupid door wouldn't open, either!

And so I kicked it. And I hanged on the handle. 'Cause I weigh thirty-seven.

"OPEN UP AND I MEAN IT!" I yelled.

But the door kept on staying shut!

"IT'S A 'MERGENCY!" I shouted.

And then all of a sudden I remembered about that boy I can beat up! 'Cause *he* had a 'mergency, too! And *he* got to go into the *boys'* bathroom!

And so I zoomed across the hall. And I pulled on the boys' bathroom door. But that dumb thing was locked, too!

"STUPID, STUPID DOORS!" I hollered.

After that, I started to jiggle up and down very fast. "OH, NO! NOW I'M GONNA HAVE AN ACCIDENT ON MY SKIRT THAT LOOKS LIKE VELVET!"

Only just then I remembered something *else* about 'mergencies. 'Cause Mother told me what to do if I ever needed help.

And its name is Call 911!

And so then I ran back to the dangerous nurse's office. 'Cause that's where the phone was, of course! And then I picked it up. And I pushed the 9! And the 1! And another 1!

"HELP! THIS IS A 'MERGENCY!" I yelled. "ALL THE DOORS ARE LOCKED IN THIS PLACE! AND NOW I'M GOING TO HAVE A TERRIBLE ACCIDENT!"

Then I heard a voice on the other end. She said for me to calm down.

"YEAH, ONLY I CAN'T! 'Cause I'M IN BIG TROUBLE! AND I'M ALL BY MYSELF! AND I NEED HELP REAL BAD!"

Then the lady said to calm down again. Except for I couldn't stand still! And so I just hung up and ran right out of there.

And I just kept running and running till I got to the big doors at the end of the hall.

And then I runned right outside! 'Cause maybe there might be a little toilet out there or something.

Except I didn't see one. All I could hear

was sirens! Loud sirens were all over the place.

And they kept on getting closer and closer! And then a big green fire truck came zooming right around the corner! And a white police car! And a fast red ambulance!

And guess what else? They turned right into the school parking lot!

And so I stopped jiggling for a second.

And I sniffed the air. Only I couldn't smell any smoke!

Then I heard a grouchy voice. "HEY! HOLD IT, MISSY!" it yelled.

And I got very scared inside. 'Cause missy's my name when I'm in trouble.

I turned around. It was the man with the can! And he was running at me!

"HOLD IT RIGHT THERE!" he hollered again.

And then I started to cry.

"Yeah, only that's the trouble. I can't hold it!" I said. "I already holded it all I can! And now I'm having a 'mergency! And all the bathrooms are locked! And now I'm going to have an accident very quick!"

And then the man with the can didn't look so grouchy anymore.

"Well, why didn't you say so, sis!" he said.

Then he pulled a big bunch of keys out of his pocket. And he grabbed my hand.

And then him and me zoomed back into the school! Speedy fast!

10
Me and That Grace

The man with the can unlocked the girls' bathroom for me. And I ran right in there.

And guess what? I made it! That's what! I didn't have an accident on my skirt that looks like velvet!

"Whew! That was a close one!" I said.

Then I washed my hands at the sink. And I looked in the mirror. And the gold star was still on my forehead!

It looked very beautiful up there!

After that, I went into the hall and the

man with the can bended down to me.

"Everything okay, sis?" he said.

And so I nodded my head. "I holded it," I said very happy.

Then all of a sudden there were lots of people running at us.

There were firemen. And policemen. And there was a tall lady rolling a bed on wheels.

"Hey!" I said to the man with the can. "What happened? Did somebody get runned over in here or something?"

Then I saw Mrs. and Principal and Mother. They were running at us, too.

And then Mother bended down and hugged me very tight!

After that everyone started talking at once. And nobody was using their quiet voices. And nobody was smiling, either.

Principal started asking me a jillion questions. Mostly they were questions about hiding in the supply closet.

"I'm a good hider," I told him.

Principal acted a little bit grumpy. He said I wasn't allowed to do that anymore.

"When you go to school, you have to follow the rules," he said. "What would happen if every boy and girl hid in the supply closet after school?"

"It would be very smushy in there," I said.

Then he made his eyes frowny. "But we wouldn't know where anyone was, would we?" he said.

"Yes," I said. "We would all be in the supply closet."

Then Principal looked up at the ceiling. And I looked up, too. But I didn't see anything again.

After that, Mother looked at my Band-

Aids. "Did you hurt yourself?" she asked.

And so I told her all about the dangerous nurse's office. And then I showed her the nurse's purple sweater. And she made me give it back.

After that, everybody started leaving. The firemen. And the policemen. And also the tall lady with the bed.

Then finally, my mother got to take me home. And guess what? I didn't have to ride on the stupid smelly bus.

Except the car wasn't that fun. 'Cause Mother was grouchy at me.

"I'm sorry the bus wasn't fun for you, Junie B.," she said. "But what you did was very, very wrong. Didn't you see all the commotion you caused? You had a *lot* of people very scared."

"Yes, but I didn't want chocolate milk

poured on my head," I explained to her.

"That's *not* going to happen," growled Mother. "And you can't just suddenly decide for yourself not to ride the bus. *Hundreds* of kids ride buses every day. And if they can do it, you can do it, too."

Then my eyes got wet again. "Yeah, but there's meanies on that thing," I said all sniffly.

Then Mother stopped being so growly.

"What if you had a friend to ride with?" she said. "Your teacher told me there's a girl in your class who will be riding the bus for the first time tomorrow. Maybe you could sit together. Would you like that?"

I made my shoulders go up and down.

"Her name is Grace," said Mother.

"Grace?" I said. "Hey! I know that Grace! I learned her today!"

And so when we got home, Mother called

that Grace's mother. And then they talked. And then me and that Grace talked, too. I said hi and she said hi. And she said she would sit with me.

And so tomorrow I get to take my little red purse on the bus. And I get to put it on the seat next to me so nobody will sit there.

Nobody except for that Grace, of course.

And then she and me might get to be buddies. And we can hold hands. Just like me and Lucille.

I will like that, I think.

And guess what else?

Tomorrow I think I might like yellow a little bit, too.

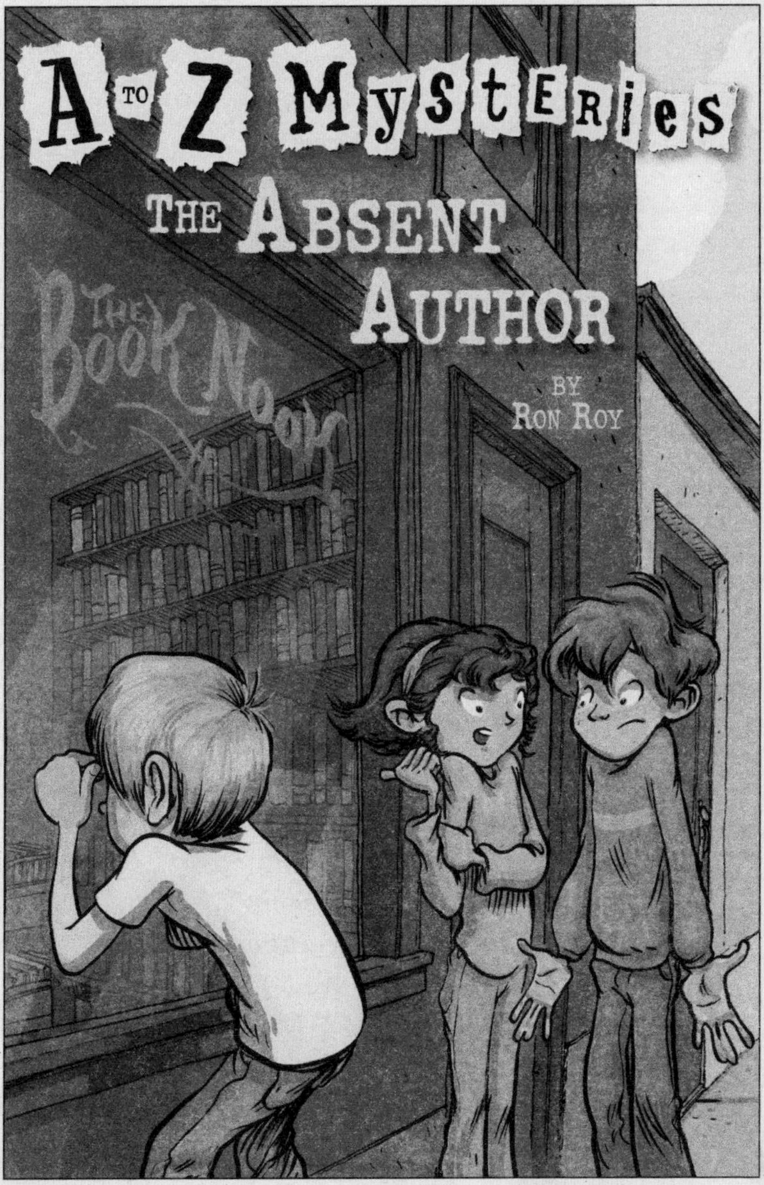
A to Z Mysteries®
THE ABSENT AUTHOR
BY
RON ROY
THE BOOK NOOK

A to Z Mysteries®

For a list of A to Z Mysteries® Super Editions,
visit rhcbooks.com

A to Z Mysteries®

The
Absent
Author

by **Ron Roy**

illustrated by
John Steven Gurney

A STEPPING STONE BOOK™

Random House  New York

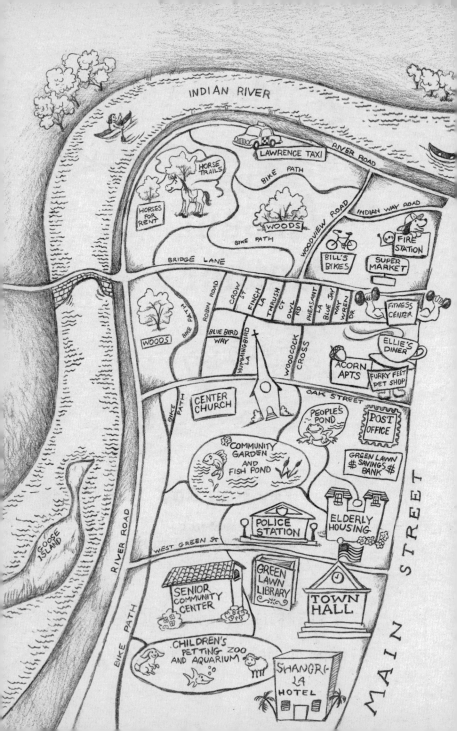

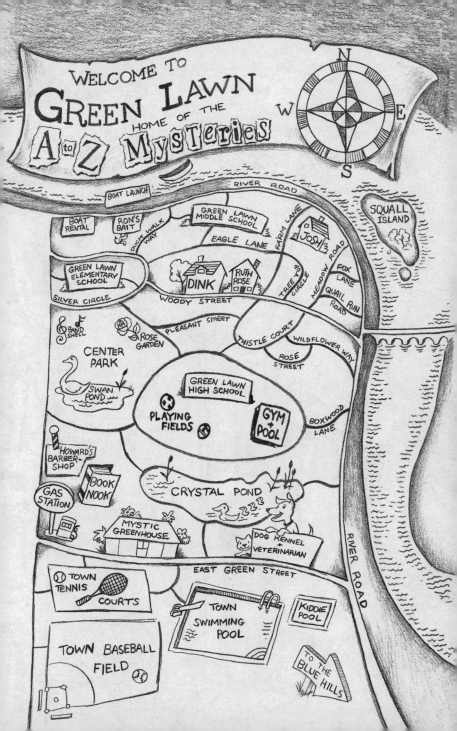

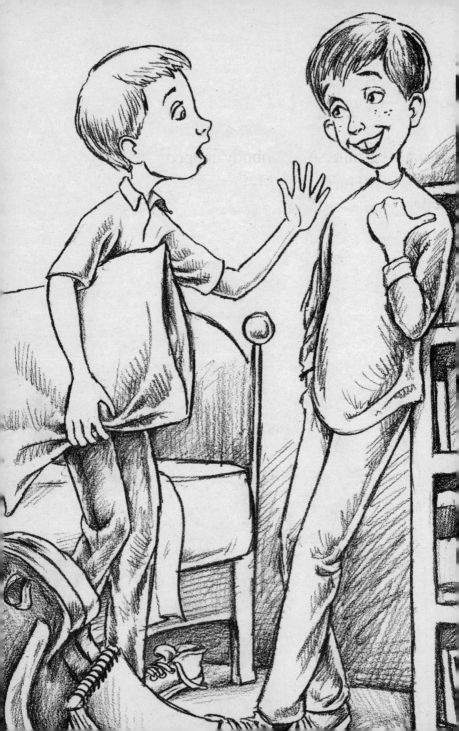

Chapter 1

"Please, Josh," Dink said. "If you come with me today, I'll owe you one. Just name it. *Anything!*"

Dink's full name was Donald David Duncan. But no one in Green Lawn ever called him that. Except his mother, when she meant business.

Josh Pinto grinned at his best friend.

"Anything?" He raised his mischievous green eyes toward the ceiling of Dink's bedroom. "Let's see, what do you have that I want?" He scratched his head. "I know, I'll take Loretta!"

Dink tossed a pillow at Josh. "When I said *anything,* I meant anything but my guinea pig! Are you coming with me or not? I have to be at the Book Nook in fifteen minutes!"

Dink rushed into the bathroom, tucking his shirt into his jeans at the same time. Josh followed him.

Standing in front of the mirror, Dink yanked a brush through his thick blond hair. "Well?" he asked. "Are you coming with me?"

"What's so important about this writer guy?" Josh asked, sitting on the edge of the bathtub.

Dink turned around and pointed his hairbrush. "Wallis Wallace isn't just

some writer guy, Josh. He's the most famous mystery writer in the world! All the kids read his books. Except for you."

"If he's so famous, why's he coming to dinky little Green Lawn?"

Dink charged back into his bedroom. "I told you! He's coming because I *invited* him. I'm scared to death to meet someone so famous. I don't even know what you're supposed to say to an author!"

Dink dived under his bed and backed out again with his sneakers. "Please come with me?"

Josh leaned in the bedroom doorway. "Sure I'll come, you dope. I'm just trying to make you sweat. Usually you're so calm!"

Dink stared at his friend. "You will? Thanks! I can't believe Wallis Wallace is really coming. When I wrote and asked him, I never thought he'd say yes."

Dink yanked his backpack out of his closet. "Pack my books, okay? I'm getting Wallis Wallace to sign them all!"

Josh began pulling Wallis Wallace books off Dink's bookshelf. "Geez, how many do you have?"

"Every one he's written." Dink sat on the floor to tie his sneakers. "Twenty-three so far. You should read some of them, Josh."

Josh picked out *The Poisoned Pond* and read the back cover. "Hey, cool! It says here that Wallis Wallace lives in a castle in Maine! Wouldn't that be neat?"

Dink grinned. "When I'm a famous writer, you can live in my castle, Josh."

"No way. When I'm a famous *artist*, you can live in *my* castle. Down in the basement!"

Josh picked up *The Riddle in the River*. "What's this guy look like?" he

asked. "And how come his picture isn't on any of these books?"

"I wondered about that, too," Dink said. "I sent him one of my school pictures and asked for one of him. But when I got his letter, there was no picture."

He finished tying his laces. "Maybe Wallis Wallace just doesn't like having his picture taken."

Josh squeezed all twenty-three books into Dink's pack. He grinned at Dink. "Or maybe he's just too ugly."

Dink laughed. "Gee, Josh, *you're* ugly and you love having your picture taken."

"Haw, haw." Josh picked up his drawing pad. "But just because you're my best friend, I'll draw his picture at the bookstore."

Dink looked at his watch. "Yikes!" he said. "We have to pick up Ruth Rose in one minute!" He tore into the bath-room and started brushing his teeth.

"How'd you get her to come?" Josh called.

Dink rushed back into his room, wiping toothpaste from his mouth. "You kidding? Ruth Rose loves Wallis Wallace's books."

Dink slung his backpack over his shoulder. He and Josh hurried next door to 24 Woody Street. Tiger, Ruth Rose's orange cat, was sitting in the sun on the steps.

Dink pressed the doorbell.

Ruth Rose showed up at the door.

As usual, she was dressed all in one color. Today it was purple. She wore purple coveralls over a purple shirt and had on purple running shoes. A purple baseball cap kept her black curls out of her face.

"Hey," she said. Then she turned

around and screamed into the house. "THE GUYS ARE HERE, MOM. I'M LEAVING!"

Dink and Josh covered their ears.

"Geez, Ruth Rose," Josh said. "I don't know what's louder, your outfit or your voice."

Ruth Rose smiled sweetly at Josh.

"I can't wait until Wallis Wallace signs my book!" she said. She held up a copy of *The Phantom in the Pharmacy*.

"I wonder if Wallis Wallace will read from the new book he's working on," Dink said.

"What's the title?" Ruth Rose asked.

They headed toward the Book Nook.

"I don't know," said Dink. "But he wrote in his letter that he's doing some of the research while he's here in Connecticut."

Dink pulled the letter out of his

pocket. He read it out loud while he walked.

Dear Mr. Duncan,

Thank you for your kind letter. I'm so impressed that you've read all my books! I have good news. I've made arrangements to come to the Book Nook to sign books. I can use part of my time for research. Thanks for your picture. I'm so happy to finally meet one of my most loyal fans. Short of being kidnapped, nothing will stop me from coming!

See you soon,

Wallis Wallace

The letter was signed *Wallis Wallace* in loopy letters. Dink grinned. "Pretty neat, huh?"

"Pretty neat, *Mister* Duncan!" teased Josh.

"You should have that letter framed," Ruth Rose said.

"Great idea!" Dink said.

They passed Howard's Barbershop. Howard waved through his window as they hurried by.

"Come on!" Dink urged as he dragged his friends down the street to the Book Nook.

They looked through the window, out of breath. The bookstore was crowded with kids. The Book Nook's owner, Mr. Paskey, had set up folding chairs. Dink noticed that most of them were already taken.

Dink saw Mr. Paskey sitting behind a table. A big white sign on the table said WELCOME, WALLIS WALLACE!

But the chair behind the sign was empty. Dink gulped and stared at the empty seat.

Where was Wallis Wallace?

Chapter 2

Dink raced into the Book Nook. Josh and Ruth Rose were right behind him. They found three seats behind Tommy Tomko and Eddie Carini.

Dink plopped his pack on the floor. The clock over the cash register said three minutes after eleven.

"Where is he?" Dink whispered to Tommy Tomko.

Tommy turned around. "Beats me. He's not here yet, and Mr. Paskey looks worried."

"What's going on?" Ruth Rose said.

Dink told her and Josh what Tommy had said.

"Paskey does look pretty nervous," Josh whispered.

"Mr. Paskey always looks nervous," Dink whispered back, looking around the room. He saw about thirty kids he knew. Mrs. Davis, Dink's neighbor, was looking at gardening books.

Dink checked out the other grownups in the store. None of them looked like a famous mystery writer.

Mr. Paskey stood up. "Boys and girls, welcome to the Book Nook! Wallis Wallace should be here any second. How many of you have books to be autographed?"

Everyone waved a book in the air.

"Wonderful! I'm sure Wallis Wallace will be happy to know that Green Lawn is a reading town!"

The kids clapped and cheered.

Dink glanced at the clock. Five past eleven. He swallowed, trying to stay calm. Wallis Wallace was late, but it was only by five minutes.

Slowly, five more minutes passed. Dink felt his palms getting damp. *Where* is *Wallis Wallace?* he wondered.

Some of the kids started getting restless. Dink heard one kid say, "Whenever *I'm* late, I get grounded!"

"So where is he?" Josh asked.

Ruth Rose looked at her watch. "It's only ten after," she said. "Famous people are always late."

Now Dink stared at the clock. The big hand jerked forward, paused, then wobbled forward again.

At 11:15, Mr. Paskey stood up again. "I don't understand why Wallis Wallace is late," he said. Dink noticed that his bald head was shiny with sweat. His bow tie was getting a workout.

Mr. Paskey smiled bravely, but his
eyes were blinking like crazy through
his thick glasses. "Shall we give him a
few more minutes?"

The crowd grumbled, but nobody
wanted to go anywhere.

Ruth Rose started to read her book.

Josh opened his sketch pad and began drawing Mr. Paskey. Dink turned and stared at the door. He mentally ordered Wallis Wallace to walk through it. *You have to come!* thought Dink.

Ever since he had received Wallis Wallace's letter, he'd thought about only one thing: meeting him today.

Suddenly Dink felt his heart skip a beat. THE LETTER! *Short of being kidnapped,* the letter said, *nothing will stop me from coming.*

Kidnapped! Dink shook himself. Of course Wallis Wallace hadn't been kidnapped!

Mr. Paskey stood again, but this time he wasn't smiling. "I'm sorry, kids," he said. "But Wallis Wallace doesn't seem to be coming after all."

The kids groaned. They got up, scraping chairs and bumping knees. Mr. Paskey apologized to them as they crowded past, heading for the door.

"I've read every single one of his books," Dink heard Amy Flower tell another girl. "Now I'll probably *never* meet anyone famous!"

"I can't believe we gave up a soccer game for this!" Tommy Tomko muttered to Eddie Carini on their way out.

Ruth Rose and Josh went next, but Dink remained in his seat. He was too stunned to move.

He felt the letter through his jeans. *Short of being kidnapped...* Finally Dink got up and walked out.

Josh and Ruth Rose were waiting for him.

"What's the matter?" Ruth Rose said. "You look sick!"

"I *am* sick," Dink mumbled. "I invited him here. It's all my fault."

"What's all your fault?" Josh asked.

"This!" he said, thrusting the letter into Josh's hands. "Wallis Wallace has been *kidnapped!*"

Chapter 3

"KIDNAPPED?" Ruth Rose shrieked. Her blue eyes were huge.

Josh and Dink covered their ears.

"Shh!" said Josh. He handed the letter back to Dink and gave a quick gesture with his head. "Some strange woman is watching us!"

Dink had noticed the woman earlier. She'd been sitting in the back of the
Book Nook.

"She's coming over here!" Ruth
Rose said.

The woman had brown hair up in a
neat bun. Half-glasses perched on her

nose. She was wearing a brown dress and brown shoes, and carried a book bag with a picture of a moose on the side. Around her neck she wore a red scarf covered with tiny black letters.

"Excuse me," she said in a soft, trembly voice. "Did you say Wallis Wallace has been *kidnapped?*" The woman poked her glasses nervously.

Dink wasn't sure what to say. He *thought* Wallis Wallace had been kidnapped, but he couldn't be sure. Finally he said, "Well, he might have been."

"My goodness!" gasped the woman.

"Who are you?" Josh asked her.

"Oh, pardon me!" The woman blushed. "My name is Mavis Green," she mumbled. "I'm a writer, and I came to meet Mr. Wallace."

Dink said, "I'm Dink Duncan. These are my friends Ruth Rose and Josh."

Mavis shook hands shyly.

Then she reached into her book bag and pulled out a folded paper.

"Wallis Wallace wrote to me last week. He said something very peculiar in his letter. I didn't think much of it at the time. But when he didn't show up today, and then I heard you mention kidnapping…"

She handed the letter to Dink. Josh and Ruth Rose read it over his shoulder.

Dear Mavis,

Thanks for your note. I'm well, and thank you for asking. But lately my imagination is playing tricks on me. I keep thinking I'm being followed! Maybe that's what happens to mystery writers—we start seeing bad guys in the shadows! At any rate, I'm eager to meet you in Green Lawn, and I look forward to our lunch after the signing.

Wallis Wallace

"Wow!" said Ruth Rose. "First he says he's being followed, and then he winds up missing!"

Dink told Mavis about his letter from Wallis Wallace. "He said the only thing that would keep him from coming today was if he was kidnapped!"

"Oh, dear!" said Mavis. "I just don't understand. Why would anyone want to kidnap Wallis Wallace?"

"If he's the most famous mystery writer in the world, he must be rich, right?" Josh said. "Maybe someone kidnapped him for a ransom!"

Suddenly Josh grabbed Dink and spun him around, pointing toward the street. "Look! The cops are coming! They must have heard about the kidnapping!"

A police officer was walking toward them.

"Josh, that's just Officer Fallon,

Jimmy Fallon's grandfather," said Dink. "Jimmy came to get a book signed. I saw him inside the Book Nook."

"Maybe we should show Officer Fallon these letters," Ruth Rose suggested. "They could be clues if Wallis Wallace has really been kidnapped!"

"Who's been kidnapped?" asked Officer Fallon, who was now standing near them. "Not my grandson, I hope," he added, grinning.

Dink showed Officer Fallon the two letters. "We think Wallis Wallace might have been kidnapped," he said. "He promised he'd come to sign books, but he isn't here."

Officer Fallon read Mavis's letter first, then Dink's. He scratched his chin, then handed the letters back.

"The letters do sound a bit suspicious," he said. "But it's more likely that Mr. Wallace just missed his flight."

Jimmy Fallon ran out of the Book Nook, waving a Wallis Wallace book at his grandfather. "Grampa, he never came! Can we go for ice cream anyway?"

Officer Fallon put a big hand on Jimmy's head. "In a minute, son." To Dink he said, "I wouldn't worry. Mr. Wallace will turn up. Call me tomorrow if there's no news, okay?"

They watched Jimmy and his grandfather walk away.

Dink handed Mavis's letter back to her. He folded his and slid it into his pocket. Crazy thoughts were bouncing around in his head. *What if Wallis Wallace really has been kidnapped? It happened because I invited him to Green Lawn. I'm practically an accomplice!*

"I don't want to wait till tomorrow," he said finally. "I say we start looking for Wallis Wallace now!"

"Where do we start?" Ruth Rose asked.

Dink jerked his thumb over his shoulder. "Right here at the Book Nook."

"Excuse me," Mavis Green said shyly. "May I come along, too?"

"Sure," Dink said. He marched back inside the Book Nook, with the others following.

Mr. Paskey was putting the Wallis Wallace books back on a shelf. He looked even more nervous than before.

"Excuse me, Mr. Paskey," Dink said. "Have you heard from Wallis Wallace?"

Mr. Paskey's hand shot up to his bow tie. "No, Dink, not a word."

"We think he was kidnapped!" Josh said.

Mr. Paskey swallowed, making his bow tie wiggle. "Now, Joshua, let's not jump to conclusions. I'm sure there's a rational explanation for his absence."

Dink told Mr. Paskey about the two letters. "I'm really worried, Mr. Paskey. Where could he be?"

Mr. Paskey took out a handkerchief and wiped his face. "I have no idea." He removed a paper from his desk and handed it to Dink. "All I have is his itinerary."

The others looked over Dink's shoulder as he read:

Itinerary for Wallis Wallace:

1. Arrive at Bradley Airport at 7:00 P.M., Friday, July 15, New England Airlines, Flight 3132.

2. Meet driver from Lawrence Taxi Service.

3. Drive to Shangri-La Hotel.

4. Sign books at Book Nook at 11:00 A.M., Saturday, July 16.

5. Lunch, then back to airport for 4:30 P.M. flight.

"Can I keep this?" Dink asked Mr. Paskey.

Mr. Paskey blinked. "Well, I guess that'll be all right. But why do you need the itinerary?"

Dink picked up a marker and drew circles around the words AIRPORT, TAXI, HOTEL, and BOOK NOOK.

"This is like a trail. It leads from the airport last night to the Book Nook today," Dink said. "Somewhere along this trail, Wallis Wallace disappeared."

Dink stared at the itinerary. "And we're going to find him!"

Chapter 4

Mr. Paskey shooed them out of the Book Nook and locked the front door. "I have to eat lunch," he said. He scurried down Main Street.

"Come on," Dink said. "There's a phone in Ellie's Diner."

"Good, we can eat while you're calling..." Josh stopped. "Who are you calling?"

"The airport," Dink said, "to see if Wallis Wallace was on that seven o'clock flight last night."

They walked into Ellie's Diner just

as Jimmy Fallon and his grandfather came out. Jimmy was working on a triple-decker chocolate cone.

Ellie stood behind the counter. As usual, her apron was smeared with ketchup, mustard, chocolate, and a lot of stuff Dink didn't recognize.

Ellie smiled. "Hi, Dink. Butter crunch, right?"

Dink shook his head. "No, thanks, Ellie. I came to use the phone."

"Excuse me, but would it be all right if I bought you each a cone?" Mavis Green asked. "I was going to buy lunch for Mr. Wallace anyway."

"Gee, thanks," Josh said. "I'll have a scoop of mint chip and a scoop of pistachio."

"Oh, you like green ice cream, too," Mavis said. She smiled shyly. "I'll have the same, please."

"I like pink ice cream," Ruth Rose

said. "I'll have a strawberry cone, please. One scoop."

"How about you, Dink?" Mavis asked.

"I'm not hungry, thanks," he said. "But you guys go ahead. I'm going to call the airport."

Dink felt guilty. If he hadn't invited
Wallis Wallace to Green Lawn, his
favorite author would be safe at home
in his castle in Maine.

But Dink couldn't help feeling excited too. He felt like a detective from one
of Wallis Wallace's books!

Dink stepped into the phone booth, looked up the number for New England Airlines, and called. When a voice came on, he asked if Wallis Wallace had been aboard Flight 3132 last night.

"He was? Did it land at seven o'clock?" Dink asked. "Thanks a lot!"

He rushed out of the phone booth. "Hey, guys, they told me Wallis Wallace was on the plane—and it landed right on time!"

"So he didn't miss his flight," Ruth Rose said through strawberry-pink lips.

"That's right!" Dink pulled out the itinerary. He drew a line through AIRPORT.

"This is so exciting!" Ruth Rose said.

"Now what?" Josh asked, working on his double-dipper.

Dink pointed to his next circle on the itinerary. "Now we need to find out if a taxi picked him up," he said.

"Lawrence Taxi is over by the river," Ruth Rose said.

Dink looked at Mavis. "Would you like to come with us? We can walk there in five minutes."

Mavis Green wiped her lips carefully with a napkin. "I'd love to come," she said in her soft voice.

They left Ellie's Diner, walked left on Bridge Lane, then headed down Woodview Road toward the river.

"Mr. Paskey looked pretty upset, didn't he?" Josh said, crunching the last of his cone. His chin was green.

"Wouldn't you be upset if you had a bunch of customers at your store waiting to meet a famous author and he didn't show up?" Ruth Rose asked.

"Yeah, but he was sweating buckets," Josh said. "I wonder if Mr. Paskey kidnapped Wallis Wallace."

"Josh, get real! Why would Mr.

Paskey kidnap an author?" asked Ruth Rose. "He sells tons of Wallis Wallace's books!"

"I don't think Mr. Paskey is the kidnapper," Dink said. "But in a way, Josh is right. Detectives should consider everyone a suspect, just the way they do in Wallis Wallace's books."

At River Road, they turned left. Two minutes later, Dink pushed open the door of the Lawrence Taxi Service office. He asked the man behind the counter if one of their drivers had met Flight 3132 at Bradley Airport the previous night.

The man ran his finger down a list on a clipboard. "That would be Maureen Higgins. She's out back eating her lunch," he said, pointing over his shoulder. "Walk straight through."

They cut through the building to a grassy area in back. Through the trees,

Dink could see the Indian River. The sun reflected off the water like bright coins.

A woman was sitting at a picnic table eating a sandwich and filling in a crossword puzzle.

"Excuse me, are you Maureen Higgins?" Dink asked.

The woman shook her head without looking up. "Nope, I'm Marilyn Monroe."

The woman wrote in another letter. Then she looked up. She had the merriest blue eyes Dink had ever seen.

"Yeah, cutie pie, I'm Maureen." She pointed her sandwich at Dink. "And who might you be?"

"I'm Dink Duncan," he said. "These are my friends Josh, Ruth Rose, and Mavis."

"We wondered if you could help us," Ruth Rose said.

Maureen stared at them. "How?"

"Did you pick up a man named Wallis Wallace at the airport last night?" Dink asked.

Maureen squinted one of her blue eyes. "Why do you want to know?"

"Because he's missing!" said Josh.

"Well, I sure ain't got him!" Maureen took a bite out of her sandwich. Mayonnaise oozed onto her fingers.

"I know. I mean, we didn't think you had him," Dink said. "But did you pick him up?"

Maureen nodded, swallowing. "Sure I picked him up. Seven o'clock sharp, I was there with my sign saying WALLACE. The guy spots me, trots over, I take him out to my taxi. He climbs in, carrying a small suitcase. Kinda spooky guy. Dressed in a hat, long raincoat, sunglasses. Sunglasses at night! Doesn't speak a word, just sits. Spooky!"

"Did you take him to the Shangri-la Hotel?" Dink asked.

"Yep. Those were my orders. Guy didn't have to give directions, but it woulda been nice if he'd said something. Pass the time, you know? Lotta people, they chat just to act friendly. Not this one. Quiet as a mouse in the back seat."

Maureen wiped mayonnaise from her fingers and lips. "Who is this Wallace fella, anyway?"

"He's a famous writer!" Ruth Rose said.

Maureen's mouth fell open. "You mean I had a celebrity in my cab and never even knew it?"

"What happened when you got to the hotel?" Josh asked.

Maureen stood up and tossed her napkin into the trash. "I get out of my side, then I open his door. He hops out,

hands me a twenty. Last I seen, he's scooting into the lobby."

Dink pulled out the itinerary. He crossed out TAXI with a thick black line. Then he drew a question mark next to HOTEL.

"Thanks a lot, Miss Higgins," he said. "Come on, guys, I have a feeling we're getting closer to finding Wallis Wallace."

Maureen put her hand on Dink's arm. "I just thought of something," she said. "When he handed me my fare, this Wallace fella was smiling."

Dink stared at Maureen. "Smiling?"

She nodded. "Yep. Had a silly grin on his face. Like he knew some big secret or something."

Chapter 5

Back on Main Street, Dink adjusted his backpack and led the way to the Shangri-la Hotel.

"Maureen Higgins said she dropped him off at the hotel last night," he told the others, "so that's our next stop."

"What if she didn't?" Josh said, catching up to Dink.

"What do you mean?"

"I mean maybe Maureen Higgins wasn't telling the truth. Maybe *she* kidnapped him!"

"And she's hiding him in her lunch-

box!" Ruth Rose said.

"Very funny, Ruth Rose," Josh said. "Maureen Higgins said she drove Wallis Wallace to the hotel. But what if she drove him somewhere else?"

"You could be right," Dink said. "That's why we're going to the hotel."

With Dink in the lead, the four approached the check-in counter in the hotel lobby.

"Excuse me," Dink said to the man behind the counter.

"May we help you?" He was the saddest-looking man Dink had ever seen. He had thin black hair and droopy eyebrows. His skinny mustache looked like a sleeping centipede. A name tag on his suit coat said MR. LINKLETTER.

"We're looking for someone."

Mr. Linkletter stared at Dink.

"He's supposed to be staying in this hotel," Josh said.

The man twitched his mustache at Josh.

"His name is Wallis Wallace," Dink explained. "Can you tell us if he checked in last night?"

Mr. Linkletter patted his mustache. "Young sir, if we had such a guest, we wouldn't give out any information. We have *rules* at the Shangri-la," he added in a deep, sad voice.

"But he's missing!" Ruth Rose said. "He was supposed to be at the Book Nook this morning and he never showed up!"

Dink pulled out the itinerary. "See, he was coming here from the airport. The taxi driver said she saw him walk into this lobby."

"And he's famous!" Ruth Rose said. She placed her book on the counter in front of Mr. Linkletter. "He wrote this!"

Sighing, Mr. Linkletter looked down

at Ruth Rose. "We are quite aware of who Mr. Wallace is, young miss."

Mr. Linkletter turned his sad eyes back on Dink. He flipped through the hotel register, glanced at it, then quickly shut the book. "Yes, Mr. Wallace checked in," he said. "He arrived at 8:05."

"He did? What happened after that?" Dink asked.

Mr. Linkletter pointed toward a bank of elevators. "He went to his room. We offered to have his suitcase carried, but he preferred to do it himself."

"Have you seen Mr. Wallace yet today?" Mavis asked.

"No, madam, I haven't seen him. Mr. Wallace is still in his room."

Still in his room!

Suddenly Dink felt relieved. He felt a little foolish, too. Wallis Wallace hadn't been kidnapped after all. He was probably in his room right now!

"Can you call him?" Dink asked.

Mr. Linkletter tapped his fingers on the closed hotel register. He patted his mustache and squinted his eyes at Dink.

"Please?" Dink said. "We just want to make sure he's okay."

Finally Mr. Linkletter turned around. He stepped a few feet away and picked up a red telephone.

As soon as his back was turned, Josh grabbed the hotel register. He quickly found yesterday's page. Dink and the others crowded around Josh for a peek.

Dink immediately recognized Wallis Wallace's signature, scrawled in big loopy letters. He had checked in to Room 303 at five after eight last night.

Dink pulled out his letter from Wallis Wallace and compared the two

signatures. They were exactly the same.

Josh dug his elbow into Dink's side. "Look!" he whispered.

Josh was pointing at the next line in the register. ROOM 302 had been printed there. Check-in time was 8:15.

"Someone else checked in right after

Wallis Wallace!" Ruth Rose whispered.

"But the signature is all smudged," Dink said. "I can't read the name."

When Mr. Linkletter hung up the phone, Josh shoved the register away.

As Mr. Linkletter turned back around, Dink shut the register. He looked up innocently. "Is he in his room?" Dink asked.

"I don't know." Mr. Linkletter tapped his fingers on his mustache. "There was no answer."

Dink's stomach dropped. His mind raced.

If Wallis Wallace had checked into his room last night, why hadn't he shown up at the Book Nook today?

And why wasn't he answering his phone?

Maybe Wallis Wallace had been kidnapped after all!

Chapter 6

Dink stared at Mr. Linkletter. "No answer? Are you sure?"

Mr. Linkletter nodded. He looked puzzled. "Perhaps he's resting and doesn't want to be disturbed."

"Can we go up and see?" Ruth Rose smiled sweetly at Mr. Linkletter. "Then we'd know for sure."

Mr. Linkletter shook his head. "We cannot disturb our guests, young miss. We have *rules* at the Shangri-la. Now good day, and thank you."

Ruth Rose opened her mouth. "But, Mis—"

"Good day," Mr. Linkletter said firmly again.

Dink and the others walked toward the door.

"Something smells fishy," muttered Dink.

"Yeah," Josh said, "and I think it's that Linkletter guy. See how he tried to hide the register? Then he turned his back. Maybe he didn't even call Room 303. Maybe he was warning his partners in crime!"

"What are you suggesting, Josh?" Mavis asked.

"Maybe Mr. Linkletter is the kidnapper," Josh said. "He was the last one to see Wallis Wallace."

A man wearing a red cap tapped Dink on the shoulder. "Excuse me, but I overheard you talking to my boss, Mr.

Linkletter. Maybe I can help you find Wallis Wallace. My kids love his books."

"Great!" Dink said. "Can you get us into his room?"

The man shook his head. "No, but I know the maid who cleaned the third-floor rooms this morning. Maybe she noticed something."

With his back to Mr. Linkletter, the man scribbled a few words on a pad and handed the page to Dink. "Good luck!" the man whispered, and hurried away.

"What'd he write?" Josh asked.

"Outside," Dink said.

They all shoved through the revolving door. In front of the hotel, Dink looked at the piece of paper. "The maid's name is Olivia Nugent. She lives at the Acorn Apartments, Number Four."

"Livvy Nugent? I know her!" Ruth Rose said. "She used to be my baby-sitter."

"The Acorn is right around the corner on Oak Street," Dink said. "Let's go!"

Soon all four were standing in front of Livvy Nugent's door. She answered it with a baby in her arms. Another little kid held on to her leg and stared at Dink and the others. He had peanut butter all over his face and in his hair.

"Hi," the boy's mother said. "I'm not buying any cookies and I already get the *Green Lawn Gazette.*" She was wearing a man's blue shirt and jeans. Her brown hair stuck out from under a Yankees baseball cap.

"Livvy, it's me!" Ruth Rose said.

Olivia stared at Ruth Rose, then broke into a grin.

"Ruth Rose, you're so big! What are

you up to these days?"

"A man at the hotel gave us your name."

"What man?"

"He was sort of old, wearing a red cap," Dink said.

Livvy chuckled. "Freddy old? He's only thirty! So why did he send you to see me?"

"He told us you cleaned the rooms on the third floor this morning," Dink said. "Did you clean Room 303?"

Livvy Nugent shifted the baby to her other arm. "Randy, please stop pulling on Mommy's leg. Why don't you go finish your lunch?" Randy ran back into the apartment.

"No," Livvy told Dink. "Nobody slept in that room. The bed was still made this morning. The towels were still clean and dry. I remember because there were two rooms in a row that I

didn't have to clean—303 and 302.
Room 302 had a Do Not Disturb sign
hanging on the doorknob. So I came
home early, paid off the baby-sitter, and
made our lunches."

"But Mr. Linkletter told us Wallis

Wallace checked into Room 303 last night," Ruth Rose said.

"Not *the* Wallis Wallace? The mystery writer? My kid sister *devours* his books!"

Dink nodded. "He was supposed to sign books at the Book Nook this morning. But he never showed up!"

"We even saw his signature on the hotel register," Ruth Rose said.

"Well, Wallis Wallace might have signed in, but he never slept in that room." Livvy grinned. "Unless he's a ghost."

"I wonder if Mr. Linkletter could have made a mistake about the room number," Mavis suggested quietly.

Livvy smiled at Mavis. "You must not be from around here. Mr. Linkletter *never* makes mistakes."

"So Wallis Wallace signed in, but he didn't sleep in his room," said Dink.

"That means..."

"Someone must have kidnapped him before he went to bed!" Josh said.

Livvy's eyes bugged. "Kidnapped! Geez, Mr. Linkletter will have a fit." She imitated his voice. "We have *rules* about kidnappings at the Shangri-la!"

Everyone except Dink laughed. All he could think about was Wallis Wallace, his favorite author, kidnapped.

Suddenly a crash came from inside the apartment. "Oops, gotta run," Livvy said. "Randy is playing bulldozer with his baby sister's stroller again. I hope you find Wallis Wallace. My kid sister will die if he doesn't write another book!"

They walked slowly back to Main Street. Dink felt as though his brain was spinning around inside his head.

Now he felt certain that Wallis Wallace had been kidnapped.

But who did it? And when?

And where was Wallis Wallace being kept?

"Guys, I'm feeling confused," he said. "Can we just sit somewhere and go over the facts again?"

"Good idea," Josh said. "I always think better when I'm eating."

"I'm feeling a bit peckish, too," Mavis said. "I need a quiet cup of tea and a sandwich. Should we meet again after lunch?"

Ruth Rose looked at her watch. "Let's meet at two o'clock."

"Where?" Josh asked.

"Back at the hotel." Dink peered through the door glass at Mr. Linkletter.

"Unless Maureen Higgins and Mr. Linkletter are *both* lying," he said, "Wallis Wallace walked into the Shangri-la last night—and never came out."

Chapter
7

Dink, Josh, and Ruth Rose left Mavis at Ellie's Diner, then headed for Dink's house. Dink made tuna sandwiches and lemonade. Ruth Rose brought a bag of potato chips and some raisin cookies from her house next door.

They ate at the picnic table in Dink's backyard. Dink took a bite of his sandwich. After he swallowed, he said, "Let's go over what we know."

He moved his lemonade glass to the middle of the table. "My glass is the air-

port," he said. "We know Wallis Wallace landed."

"How do we *know* he did?" Josh asked.

"The airport told me the plane landed, Josh."

"And Maureen Higgins said she picked him up," Ruth Rose added.

"Okay, so your glass is the airport," Josh said. "Keep going, Dink."

Dink slid his sandwich plate over next to his glass. "My plate is Maureen's taxi." He put a cookie on the plate. "The cookie is Wallis Wallace getting into the taxi."

Dink slid the plate over to the opened potato chip bag. "This bag is the hotel." He walked the Wallis Wallace cookie from the plate into the bag.

Dink looked at Josh and Ruth Rose. "But what happened to Wallis Wallace after he walked into the lobby?"

"I'll tell you what happened," Josh
said. He lined up four cookies in a row.
"This little cookie is Mr. Paskey. These
three are Maureen, Mr. Linkletter, and
Olivia Nugent."

Josh looked up and waggled his eyebrows. "I think these four cookies planned the kidnapping *together!*"

Ruth Rose laughed. "Josh, Mr. Paskey and Livvy Nugent are friends of ours. Do you really think they planned this big kidnapping? And can you see Mr. Linkletter and my baby-sitter pulling off a kidnapping together?"

Josh ate a potato chip. "Well, maybe not. But *someone* kidnapped the guy!"

"Our trail led us to the hotel, and then it ended," Dink said. "What I want to know is, if Wallis Wallace isn't in his room, where is he?"

Dink nibbled on a cookie thoughtfully. "I'm getting a headache trying to sort it all out."

Ruth Rose dug in Dink's backpack and brought out three Wallis Wallace books. "I have an idea." She handed books to Dink and Josh and kept one.

"What're these for?" Dink asked.

"Josh made me think of something Wallis Wallace wrote in *The Mystery in the Museum*," Ruth Rose said. "He said the more you know about the victim, the easier it is to figure out who did the crime."

She turned to the back cover of her book. "So let's try to find out more about our victim. Listen to this." She started reading out loud. "'When not writing, the author likes to work in the garden. Naturally, Wallis Wallace's favorite color is green.'"

"Fine," said Josh, "but how does knowing his favorite color help us find him, Ruth Rose?"

"I don't know, but maybe if we read more about him, we'll discover some clues," Ruth Rose said. "What does it say on the back of your book?"

Josh flipped the book over and began

reading. "'Wallis Wallace lives in a castle called Moose Manor.'" He looked up. "We already knew he lived in a castle. I don't see any clues yet, you guys."

Ruth Rose stared at Josh. "You know, something is bugging me, but I can't figure out what it is. Something someone said today, maybe." She shook her head. "Anyway, read yours, Dink."

Dink read from the back cover of his book. "'Wallis Wallace gives money from writing books to help preserve the wild animals that live in Maine.'"

"Okay, he gives money away to save animals, lives in a castle, and grows a bunch of green stuff," Josh said, counting on his fingers. "Still no clues."

Josh took another cookie. "But I just thought of something." He began slowly munching on the cookie.

Dink raised his eyebrows. "Are you going to tell us, Josh?"

"Well, I was thinking about Room 302. Remember, someone signed the register right after Wallis Wallace checked into Room 303? And the signature was all smudged? And then Olivia Nugent—"

"—told us that Room 302 had a Do Not Disturb sign on it!" Ruth Rose interrupted. "Livvy never went into that room at all!"

Just then Dink's mother drove up the driveway. She got out of the car, waved, and started walking toward the picnic table.

"Oh, no!" Dink said. "If Mom finds out I'm trying to find a kidnapper, she won't let me out of the house! Don't say anything, okay?"

"Can't I even say hi?" Josh asked.

Dink threw a potato chip at Josh. "Say hi, then shut up about you-know-what!"

"Hi, Mrs. Duncan!" Josh said, sliding a look at Dink.

"Hi, kids. How was the book signing? Tell me all about Wallis Wallace, Dink. Is he as wonderful as you expected?"

Dink stared at his mother. He didn't want to lie. But if he told her the truth, she wouldn't let him keep looking for Wallis Wallace. And Dink had a sudden feeling that they were very close to finding him.

We can't stop now! he thought. He looked at his mother and grinned stupidly.

"Dink? Honey? Why is your mouth open?"

He closed his mouth. *Think, Dink!* he ordered himself.

Suddenly Josh knocked over his lemonade glass. The sticky cold liquid spilled into Dink's lap.

Dink let out a yowl and jumped up.

"Gee, sorry!" said Josh.

"Paper towels to the rescue!" Dink's mother ran toward the house.

"Good thinking, Josh," Dink said, wiping at his wet jeans. "But did you have to spill it on *me?* You had the whole yard!"

Josh grinned. "Some people are never satisfied. I got you out of hot water, didn't I?"

"Right into cold lemonade," Ruth Rose said.

Dink blotted his jeans with a handful of paper napkins. "Come on. Let's go meet Mavis before my mom comes back. There's something weird happening on the third floor of the Shangri-la!"

Chapter 8

Dink's jeans were nearly dry by the time they reached the hotel. Mavis was waiting out front.

"How was your lunch?" she asked timidly.

"Fine, thanks," Dink said. "We talked it over, and we think there's something fishy going on on the third floor of this hotel."

Suddenly Mavis began coughing. She held up her scarf in front of her mouth.

Dink noticed that the letters on the

scarf were tiny M's. "Are you okay?" he asked.

"Should I run in and get you some water?" asked Josh.

Mavis took off her glasses and shook her head. "No, I'm fine, thank you. Dear me, I don't know what happened! Now, what were you saying about the third floor?"

"We think Wallis Wallace may be up there," Ruth Rose said. She reminded Mavis about the smudged signature for Room 302 and the Do Not Disturb sign on the door.

Mavis replaced her eyeglasses. "Mercy! What do you think we should do?"

"Follow me!" Dink said. For the second time, they all trooped into the hotel lobby.

Mr. Linkletter watched them from behind the counter.

"Hi," Dink said. "Remember us?"

"Vividly," Mr. Linkletter said.

"Wallis Wallace checked into Room 303, right?"

"That is correct," said Mr. Linkletter.

"Well, we talked to the maid who cleaned that room," Dink went on. "She told us no one slept in it."

"You spoke to Olivia Nugent? When? How?"

"We have our ways," Josh said.

"So," Dink went on, "we think Wallis Wallace disappeared right here in this hotel."

"And Wallis Wallace is a *very* famous writer," Ruth Rose reminded Mr. Linkletter. "Millions of kids are waiting to read his next book," she added sweetly.

Mr. Linkletter's sad eyes grew large. He swallowed and his Adam's apple bobbed up and down. He rubbed his

forehead as though he had a headache.

Then Dink told Mr. Linkletter about Room 302. "Miss Nugent said there was a Do Not Disturb sign on the door."

Ruth Rose pointed to the register. "See? The signature is all smudged!"

"We think the kidnappers are hiding Wallis Wallace in that room!" Josh said.

At the word "kidnappers," Mr. Linkletter closed his eyes. He opened a drawer, took out a bottle of headache pills, and put one on his tongue.

"Just to be on the safe side, perhaps we should check both rooms, Mr. Linkletter," Mavis said quietly.

"It'll just take a minute," Dink said.

Mr. Linkletter let out a big sigh. "Very well, but this is most unusual. Things run very smoothly at the Shangrila."

They all got into the elevator. No one spoke. Dink watched Mr. Linkletter jig-

gling his bunch of keys. Mr. Linkletter
kept his eyes on the little arrow telling
them which floor they were on.

The elevator door opened on the
third floor. Mr. Linkletter unlocked
Room 303. "Most unusual," he muttered.

The room was empty and spotlessly
clean. "Strange, very strange," Mr.
Linkletter said.

They moved to Room 302, where a
Do Not Disturb sign still hung on the
doorknob.

Mr. Linkletter knocked. They all leaned toward the door.

"Listen, I hear a voice!" Josh said.

"What's it saying?" Ruth Rose asked.

Then they all heard it.

The voice was muffled, but it was definitely yelling, "HELP!"

9

Mr. Linkletter unlocked the door and shoved it open.

A man with curly blond hair stared back at them. He was sitting in a chair with his feet tied in front of him. His arms were tied behind his back. A towel was wrapped around his mouth.

"Oh, my goodness!" Mr. Linkletter cried.

Everyone rushed into the room.

Dink ran behind the chair to untie the man's hands while Josh untied his

feet.

Mavis unwrapped the towel from around his face.

"Thank goodness you got here!" the man said. "I'm Wallis Wallace. Someone knocked on my door last night. A voice said he was from room service. When I opened the door, two men dragged me in here and tied me up."

He looked at Dink. "You're Dink Duncan! I recognize you from the picture you sent. How did you find me?"

"We followed your itinerary," Dink said. He showed Mr. Wallace the sheet of paper. "We got it from Mr. Paskey and used it as a trail. The trail led us to this room!"

"I'm so sorry I missed the book signing," Wallis Wallace said. "As you can see, I was a bit tied up."

He smiled. Then he rubbed his jaw. "My mouth is sore from that towel. I

can't believe I was kidnapped! And I can't wait to get back to my safe little cottage in Maine."

"Can you describe the two guys who kidnapped you?" Dink asked. "We should tell Officer Fallon so he can try to find them."

Wallis Wallace stared at Dink. "The two guys? Oh...well, um, I don't think I'll—"

"HEY!" Ruth Rose suddenly yelled.

Everyone looked at her.

"What's the matter?" asked Dink. "You look funny, Ruth Rose."

Ruth Rose was staring at the red scarf draped around Mavis's neck. She pointed at the man who'd been tied up. "You're not Wallis Wallace!"

Then she looked at Mavis Green. "*You* are," she said quietly.

Chapter 10

"Ruth Rose, what are you talking about?" Josh said.

Dink didn't know what to think, except that he was getting a headache.

"What makes you think *I'm* Wallis Wallace?" Mavis asked.

Ruth Rose walked over to Mavis. "May I borrow your scarf?" she said.

Ruth Rose held the scarf up so everyone could see it. "When I first saw this scarf, I thought these little black letters were M's," she said. "M for Mavis."

She looked at Mavis Green. "But they're not M's, are they?"

She turned the scarf completely upside down. "What do they look like now?"

Dink stepped closer. "They're little W's now!"

"Right. Double-U, double-U for *Wallis Wallace!*" Ruth Rose pointed at the man. "You just said you live in a little cottage. But Wallis Wallace lives in a big *castle* in Maine. It says so on the cover of *The Silent Swamp.*"

Ruth Rose pointed at Mavis's book bag. "Seeing your bag again made me remember something I thought of today. Josh read that your castle was called Moose Manor. There's a picture of a moose on the side of your bag."

Ruth Rose handed the scarf back to Mavis. "And we read that Wallis Wallace's favorite color is green. You like green ice cream, and you chose Mavis Green for your fake name."

Everyone was staring at Ruth Rose, except for the man they had untied. He started laughing.

"The cat's out of the bag now, sis," he said.

Then Mavis laughed and gave Ruth Rose a hug.

"Yes, Ruth Rose," Mavis said. "I really *am* Wallis Wallace." She put her hand on the man's shoulder. "And this is my brother, Walker Wallace. We've been planning my 'kidnapping' for weeks!"

Dink stared at Mavis, or whoever she was. "You mean Wallis Wallace is a woman?" he said.

"Yes, Dink, I'm a woman, and I'm definitely Wallis Wallace." She winked at him. "Honest!"

Mavis, the real Wallis Wallace, sat on the bed. She took off her glasses and

pulled the barrettes out of her hair. She shook her hair until it puffed out in a mass of wild curls.

"Thank goodness I can be myself now!" she said. "All day I've had to act like timid Mavis Green. I can't wait to get out of this fuddy-duddy dress and into my jeans again!"

She kicked off her shoes and wiggled her toes in the air. "Boy, does that feel good!"

Dink blinked and shook his head. Mavis Green was really Wallis Wallace? He couldn't believe it. "But why did you pretend to be kidnapped?" he asked.

The real Wallis Wallace grinned at the kids' surprised faces. "I owe you an explanation," she said.

"My new book is about a children's mystery writer who gets kidnapped. In my book, some children rescue the

writer. I wanted to find out how *real* kids might solve the mystery," she explained.

She smiled at Dink. "Then your letter came, inviting me to Green Lawn. That's what gave me the idea to fake my own kidnapping. I'd become Mavis Green and watch what happened."

"Oh, yeah!" Dink said. "In your let-

ter, you said you were doing some research in Connecticut."

She nodded. "Yes, and I mentioned the word 'kidnap' in the letter to get you thinking along those lines." She smiled at the three kids. "I thought I'd have to give you more clues, but you solved the mystery all by yourselves!"

Dink laughed. "You recognized me in

the bookstore from my picture," he said. "And you didn't send *me* a picture so I wouldn't recognize *you!*"

"Then my nutty sister dragged *me* into her plan," Walker Wallace said. "I should be home checking my lobster pots."

"While you were eating lunch, Walker and I ate ours up here," Wallis said. "Then, just before two o'clock, I tied him in the chair and ran downstairs to meet you out front as Mavis."

Wallis Wallace threw back her head and laughed. "Do you remember downstairs when Dink said there was something fishy on the third floor?"

She got up and stood next to her brother. "Well, I'm always teasing Walker about smelling fishy from handling his lobster bait. So when you said something was *fishy* in the hotel, I had to pretend to cough so you wouldn't

know I was really laughing!"

"Boy, did you have us fooled," Dink said.

Wallis Wallace grinned. "Mr. Paskey was in on it. I had to tell him the truth. As you saw this morning at the Book Nook, my little scheme made him very nervous. I've promised him I'll come back and do a real book signing soon. But I'll be in disguise, so be prepared for anything!"

Dink shook his head. "I was so disappointed because I couldn't meet my favorite author this morning," he said. "And I've been with you all day and didn't even know it!"

She looked at Dink. "I'm so sorry I tricked you. Will you forgive me?"

Dink blushed. "Sure."

"I have a question," Josh said. "Where did you really sleep last night?"

"Right here in Room 302. A few

weeks ago, I telephoned to reserve two rooms next to each other. Last night, I checked into Room 303 as Wallis Wallace, the man. Up in Room 303, I took off the hat and coat and sunglasses. Then I sneaked back down to the lobby wearing a blond wig. I checked in again, this time into Room 302."

"Did you smudge the signature?" Ruth Rose asked.

"Oh, you noticed that!" Wallis said. "I'm so used to signing my real name in books, I started to write *Wallis*. So I 'accidentally' smudged it."

"I have a question, Mavis, I mean Miss Wallace...what should we call you?" Dink asked.

"My friends call me Wallis," she said.

"Well, the taxi driver told us you were smiling in the taxi. What were you smiling about?"

Wallis Wallace was smiling now.

"Oh, about a lot of things. First, I was wearing a man's disguise, and that made me feel pretty silly. And I knew I was going to meet you, one of my biggest fans. And I was happy because I knew whatever happened, the next day would be fun!"

"I sure had fun," Josh said, grinning. "Poor Mr. Paskey, having to lie to everyone with a straight face!"

"Boy, did I have a hard time pretending to be Mavis all day," Wallis said. "But my plan worked. I met three brilliant detectives. You helped me to see how real kids would investigate a kidnapping. Now I can go back to Maine and finish my book."

"How come your book jackets never say that you're a woman?" Ruth Rose asked.

Wallis Wallace smiled. "Because of my name, most people assume that I'm a man," she explained. "I let them think that so I can do my research easier. I've learned that people clam up if they know I'm Wallis Wallace. So out in public I pretend I'm Mavis Green, just a regular person, not a mystery writer."

"I get it!" Dink said. "You don't have your picture on your books so people can't recognize you."

"Right. And I hope you'll keep my secret."

"We will. Right, guys?" Ruth Rose said.

"Thank you! Any more questions?" Wallis asked.

"Yeah," Walker said, giving his sister a look. "When do we leave? I've got lobsters waiting for me."

"I have a question, too," Dink said. "Will you send me your picture now?"

"Yes, but I'll do better than that," Wallis said. "I'll dedicate my next book

to my three new friends!"

Dink, Josh, and Ruth Rose did a triple high five.

"Excuse me," Mr. Linkletter said from the door where he had been standing.

They all looked at him.

"It's nearly checkout time."

Everyone laughed.

Mr. Linkletter smiled, but just a little.

PuRRmaids

1

The Scaredy Cat

Sudipta Bardhan-Quallen

Swim into more

PuRRmaids

adventures!

PuRRmaiDs

1

The Scaredy Cat

by Sudipta Bardhan-Quallen

illustrations by Vivien Wu

A STEPPING STONE BOOK™

Random House New York

It was a paw-sitively beautiful morning in Kittentail Cove. Coral was very excited. After waiting all summer, it was finally the first day of sea school!

Coral carefully brushed her orange fur. She chose a sparkly headband to wear. Then she snapped a bracelet on her paw. It was her favorite because of the golden sea-shell charm. It matched the ones Angel and Shelly had.

Angel, Shelly, and Coral had been friends fur-ever. They met when they were tiny kittens. On the outside, they looked very different. They often had different ideas about what to do, where to go, and how much trouble they should get into. But somehow their differences made them purr-fect partners. Coral couldn't imagine being without Angel and Shelly.

In fact, one of her favorite things about school was that she got to be with her best friends all day.

Coral grabbed her bag and went to the door. "Bye, Papa! Bye, Mama!" she called. "See you later!"

"Good luck, Coral," Papa answered. "Don't

forget that you, Angel, and Shelly are coming here after school."

"I know, Papa," Coral replied. With a wave goodbye, she swam off. She was meeting Angel and Shelly in Leondra's Square, under the statue of Leondra, the founder of Kittentail Cove.

Purrmaids lived in every part of every ocean. They had towns in coves, reefs, and anywhere else that was beautiful and peaceful. Kittentail Cove was the best purrmaid town in the world! At least, Coral thought so.

"I hope Angel and Shelly are there already!" Coral purred. Shelly was usually on time, but Angel often ran late. The sooner they met up, the sooner they'd get to school to meet their new teacher. Coral was excited to see who it would be.

Besides, the first day of school was a terrible time to be late!

As she swam toward the statue, Coral saw Shelly. Even from far away, Shelly looked lovely. Every strand of her white fur was purr-fectly in place. She had a small starfish clip near her ear, and the golden seashell charm on her bracelet glittered.

"Shelly!" Coral called. "Have you seen Angel?"

Shelly looked up and waved to Coral. She started to say, "No, I haven't—"

"I'm right here!" someone shouted.

It was Angel! Coral spun around to face her friend.

Like Coral and Shelly, Angel was dressed up for the first day of school. She was wearing a necklace of red star-fish. The red looked beautiful against her black-and-white fur. And just like her best friends, Angel wore her golden sea-shell bracelet.

"What are you two waiting for?" Angel asked as she swam past her friends. "We have to swim to school!"

Coral bit back a smile. "You were late—and now you're telling *us* to hurry?"

Shelly laughed. "We'd better catch up. We don't want to miss the bell!"

When the girls arrived at sea school, Angel groaned. "Coral! We're early! No one else is even here yet!"

Coral giggled. "It's better to be early than late."

"But I could have slept longer!" Angel whined.

Shelly patted Angel's paw. "Since we're here, let's find our classroom," she suggested.

Angel scowled for a moment. But then she nodded. "Room Sea-Seven, right?" she asked.

"No, silly." Coral laughed. "That was our classroom *last* year!"

"We're in Eel-Twelve this year," Shelly added.

They made their way toward Eel-Twelve. There was a purrmaid inside the classroom when they arrived. She didn't look like most of the purrmaids in town. Her long fur was dyed every color of the rainbow. She wore three earrings on her left ear and four on her right. Even her tail was decorated with shiny rings!

"Is that our *teacher*?" Angel whispered.

"I think so," Coral answered.

"I've never seen a teacher who looks like that," Shelly said. "She's so cool!"

"Let's go meet her!" Angel suggested.

The girls swam into the classroom. The colorful purrmaid had her back to the door, but she spun around as the girls entered. "I thought I heard some curious little kittens," she said. "You're here early. You must love school!"

"We do!" said all three friends at once.

Their teacher grinned. "I'm glad to hear that. I'm Ms. Harbor, and today is my first day, too."

"I'm Coral," said Coral, "and these are my friends, Angel and Shelly."

"It's lovely to meet you all," Ms. Harbor purred.

The bell rang, so the purrmaids swam to their clamshell seats. Ms. Harbor welcomed more students into the classroom. Then she swam to her giant scallop-shell teacher's chair. "Let's begin, class!" she said.

There was so much to do on the first day of school that Coral lost track of time. She was surprised when Ms. Harbor announced, "Our first day is almost over, but I have some homework for you tonight."

All the students groaned. "Homework!" Angel said. "Already?"

Ms. Harbor held her paws up for silence. "This homework isn't hard, I purr-omise. In fact, you might enjoy it." She floated to the middle of the classroom. "I want to tell you something about me. I love curiosity! Curious purrmaids are not afraid to learn. That's how you find the most interesting things in the ocean!"

Coral nodded. She loved exploring the ocean, too—as long as the exploring part wasn't too scary.

"I am very excited to be your teacher this year," Ms. Harbor continued. "We are going to have a fin-tastic time learning from each other and making waves in Kittentail Cove! To start our year, I'd like each of you to bring something special to class tomorrow."

"What do you mean by 'special'?" Angel asked.

"It can be anything you want!" Ms. Harbor laughed. "Your favorite shell, a beautiful pearl, a pet sea horse. Whatever will show me how you see life's beauty. Help me learn about you!"

2

Coral always felt like she had to swim twice as fast to keep up with Angel and Shelly. But on the way home from school, it was a lot harder than usual. Angel zipped through the streets toward Coral's house so quickly that even Shelly fell behind.

"Slow down, Angel!" Shelly shouted. But Angel didn't stop.

"Don't even try," Coral said. "Angel is excited about something. And when she's excited, nothing makes her slow down!"

"What do you think is going on?" Shelly asked.

Coral shrugged. "I don't know. But I bet it has to do with our homework."

Angel didn't wait for Coral to finish hugging Mama before she asked a question. "What are you two going to do about the homework assignment?"

"Hello to you, too, Angel," Mama said.

Angel mumbled, "Hello, Mrs. Marsh."

Mama smiled. "The first day of school must have gone really well if you are this excited about homework!"

"It did!" the friends answered at the same time.

"I'm glad," Mama said. "Have fun doing your homework."

Coral kissed Mama's cheek. Then she waved for her friends to follow her to her bedroom. "This is what I'm going to bring," she announced. She held up a pink pointy turret shell. "This one is my favorite."

"It's beautiful," Shelly cooed.

"How about you?" Coral asked.

Shelly scratched her head. "I'm not sure. Maybe my red sea-glass necklace?"

Coral grinned. "I've never seen anyone else with sea glass that color. I think that would be purr-fect!"

Angel frowned. "We can't just bring in seashells and sea glass!" she moaned. "We need something better!"

Coral and Shelly looked at each other. "Like what, Angel?" Coral asked.

"I don't know. But it has to be really different and special," Angel replied.

"What if we look around Leondra's Square today?" Shelly suggested. "We could each find something new."

"That's a great idea!" Coral agreed.

"No, it's not!" Angel cried. "Remember what Ms. Harbor said about curiosity? And about finding the most interesting things in the ocean?"

Her friends nodded.

"We aren't going to find anything amazing in Leondra's Square!" Angel continued. "We want things that the other purrmaids won't be able to find. We have to look somewhere no one else will think to look."

"But where are we supposed to go?" Shelly asked.

"I don't know," Angel replied.

"Let's have a snack," Coral said, "and we can think about it."

The girls swam into the kitchen. Mama had set out some of Coral's favorite sushi to share with her best friends. They floated around the counter and popped the sushi into their mouths with their paws.

"Don't let Mama see us," Coral said between bites. "She likes us to eat at the table."

Angel rolled her eyes. "Coral," she moaned.

"I'm sorry!" Coral sighed. "I don't like breaking the rules!"

Shelly and Angel laughed. They already knew that about their friend. Coral was definitely the most careful one in their group. Angel, on the other paw, wasn't much like her name at all. She loved to bend the rules. Shelly liked adventure, too—but not if it meant getting her paws dirty, and only when she didn't have to break *too* many rules.

Angel popped another piece of sushi into her mouth. Then her face lit up. "I have an idea!" she cried. "If we head out to the edges of Kittentail

Cove, there will be lots to discover. We can search Tortoiseshell Reef for something to bring to school!"

Coral gulped. Kittentail Cove was a big place, and Tortoiseshell Reef was as far away from home as they could go. Angel's plans were always exciting, but they were also complicated—and sometimes dangerous. From the way Angel was grinning, Coral knew that this plan would be no different.

"Maybe we should think about this some more," Coral began. "I mean . . . it might not be safe to go so far. There could be strong currents! And it's really close to where barracudas and giant squids and sharks hang out!"

"We'll stay away from the sharks, silly!" Angel answered. "You're paw-some at avoiding danger, right?"

Shelly agreed with Angel. But Coral shook her head and said, "I don't think this is a good idea."

"Okay! Okay!" Angel huffed. "If you don't want to try, we'll do something else."

Coral clenched her paws. "I do want to try!" she yowled. "I'm just afraid of what could happen. Haven't you ever been scared, Angel?"

Shelly swam between Coral and Angel. "You two shouldn't fight. We're best friends!" She turned to Angel and said, "It is a really great idea to search away from the center of Kittentail Cove. I bet Ms. Harbor would be really impressed by that. But Coral has a good point, too. Maybe we should think about this some more."

Shelly smiled, but Coral could see that she really wanted to go along with Angel's plan.

Then Angel said, "Well, if Coral's too much of a scaredy cat—"

"No! I can do this," Coral interrupted. She pictured Tortoiseshell Reef. She didn't know what was out there. But she was going to be brave, no matter how scary it was!

"Are you sure?" Shelly asked.

"Yes, I'm sure," Coral replied.

"Good," Angel said, "because meow is the time."

Ms. Harbor expected them to bring in something interesting tomorrow. Angel was right—it was meow or never.

"I'll race you to Tortoiseshell Reef!" Coral shouted. "Last one there is a rotten skeg!"

Coral zipped through the water. Angel and Shelly followed on her tail. In just a few minutes, they had passed Leondra's Square and were zooming toward Cove Council Hall. At first, Coral was purring with excitement. But the farther she got from home, the more butterfly fish fluttered in her tummy. What if something bad happened? What if there was a cat-tastrophe?

She tried to stop worrying. *I need to have a paw-sitive attitude,* she thought. *We're doing our homework. And then we're going straight home!*

As they reached Cove Council Hall, they saw Angel's mother, Mrs. Shore, speaking to Mayor Rivers. "Mommy!" Angel cried. She darted toward her mother to give her a hug. But she was going so fast that she spun Mrs. Shore around three times!

"Angel!" Mrs. Shore yelped. "Slow down!"

Mayor Rivers chuckled as he helped Mrs. Shore find her balance. "Angel, you've grown so big!" he said.

"And look at you two!" Mrs. Shore said to Coral and Shelly. She took their paws and gave them a squeeze. "How was the first day of school?"

"Purr-fect!" Coral replied. Angel and Shelly nodded in agreement.

"Our new teacher is Ms. Harbor," Shelly said.

"And she gave us a cool homework assignment!" Angel added. "We're supposed to bring something really special to class tomorrow."

"Is that why you're swimming so fast?" Mayor Rivers asked. "We have speed limits in this town, you know!"

Angel, Shelly, and Coral grinned. "We're going to Tortoiseshell Reef to see what interesting things we can find," Shelly said.

Mayor Rivers smiled. "I remember spending hours exploring Tortoiseshell Reef as a youth! If the reef is like it used to be, you will have lots of luck."

The girls giggled. Coral knew what her friends were thinking. Mayor Rivers was so *old*. Back in his youth, the reef must have been just a few elkhorns and sea fans!

"You know," Mrs. Shore said, "usually the most special things are the ones we hold close to our hearts."

"Does that mean we shouldn't go to Tortoiseshell Reef?" Coral asked.

"But, Mommy," Angel whined, "none of us have anything that is truly special at home! We have to go to Tortoiseshell Reef to search!" She clasped her paws and begged. "Please?"

"Just remember not to stay out too late," Mrs. Shore said. "It gets dark quicker at the edges of the cove. And the South Canary Current can get crowded in the evening." She pointed to the tall clock tower that topped Cove Council Hall. "You should all be home before dinner."

The South Canary Current flowed right past the entrance of Kittentail Cove. Most sea creatures used the current systems to get around the ocean quickly. When her parents took Coral to visit her cousins in other purrmaid towns, they used the South Canary Current. But Coral had forgotten that the current ran along the border of Tortoiseshell Reef.

"We'll be careful, Mrs. Shore," Shelly said.

"And we'll be back by dinnertime," Angel said.

"Good," Mrs. Shore replied. "I don't want you to run into any trouble on your adventure."

Coral gulped. That's what she was afraid of, too! But there was no way she was going to say so. She didn't want to be called a scaredy cat again.

"We won't, Mommy!" Angel agreed.

The three purrmaids swam off. Soon they arrived at Tortoiseshell Reef. They gazed around at the beautiful scenery.

"Don't you just love it here?" Shelly whispered.

Coral nodded. There were houses all over Kittentail Cove. Most purrmaids lived near Leondra's Square like Coral, Shelly, and Angel. Some lived farther out, especially the pearl farmers. There were many offices and restaurants near Cove Council Hall. Coral's father worked in one of those offices. So did Angel's mother. Shelly's parents had a restaurant there, too. But no one was allowed to build on Tortoiseshell Reef. The purrmaids of Kittentail Cove set it aside as a place to enjoy the ocean's natural beauty.

"I don't know why we don't come here more often," Angel said. She darted behind an elkhorn and disappeared.

"Angel?" Coral called. "Where are you?"

Angel popped up from behind a huge sea fan. "Here I am!" she shouted.

Coral yelped and hid behind Shelly.

"Coral!" Angel said. "You weren't scared, were you?"

"Of course I wasn't scared," Coral lied, "just surprised."

Shelly patted Coral's paw and said, "It's all right. Angel surprised me, too."

"I'm sorry," Angel apologized. She put her paw around Coral and led her toward the sea fan. "Can you help me with something?" she asked. When Coral nodded, Angel said, "I don't remember all the different creatures who live here in Tortoiseshell Reef. You know them better than I do. Will you show me?"

Coral smiled. Angel was a good friend. Together, they swam toward the floor of the reef. Coral pointed out different animals.

"That's a butterfly fish," Coral said. "And that is a cleaner shrimp."

"Cleaner than what?" Angel joked. The two purrmaids giggled.

"Look over here!" Shelly called. She was looking at something hiding inside a sea whip.

Coral swam closer to get a better look. She saw a beautiful orange-and-white fish zipping between the fronds of the sea whip. "It's a clown fish!" she whispered.

"Where's the rest of the circus?" Shelly laughed.

The clown fish didn't find the joke very funny. He swam away.

The purrmaids paddled slowly around the reef. Coral showed her friends all sorts of animals and plants. She spotted a family of sea horses. "Let's take a closer look," Coral suggested.

"Great idea!" Shelly agreed.

Coral looked over her shoulder. She started to wave to Angel. But Angel wasn't there!

Coral gasped. "Where is she?"

Shelly spun around. Coral knew she couldn't see Angel, either.

"Angel!" Coral yelled. "Where are you?" Her heart began to pound. *I knew something terrible would happen,* she thought.

Coral and Shelly kept shouting their friend's name. Finally, they reached the edge of Tortoiseshell Reef. The coral there had formed a deep tunnel. "Be careful near the tunnel," Coral warned Shelly. "Sometimes eels live in those!"

Suddenly, something came whooshing out of the tunnel. Without thinking, Coral swam in front of Shelly. She closed her eyes and braced herself for whatever was coming her way.

Then Coral heard giggling. She opened one eye. "Angel!" she yelped. "You scared me!"

"You scared me, too," Shelly added.

"We thought you were an eel!" Coral said. She was still trembling from fear.

"If you thought I was an eel," Angel said, "why did you swim in front of Shelly instead of swimming away?"

"I was—I was trying to protect her," Coral stammered.

Angel grinned. "You're not such a scaredy cat after all!"

Shelly gave Coral a hug. "That was pretty brave, Coral."

Coral smiled. "I guess it was," she said.

"Well, I have something else for you to be brave about," Angel said. She pointed to the tunnel. "It's the coolest thing. On the other side of the tunnel, there's a geyser that spins you head over tail. If you swim through really fast, it will flip you over and turn you around. Then you can swim back."

"That sounds so exciting!" Shelly said.

"Let's all do it!" Angel suggested.

"I—I don't know." Coral pulled back from her friends. "What if I can't do it and get stuck upside down? What if I sink? What if . . . ?" She hung her head in embarrassment.

"Haven't you ever tried a flip?" Angel asked. "I've been doing them since I was the size of a minnow!"

Coral felt as small as a grain of sand on the ocean floor. "No, I guess I haven't ever tried."

"We can help you," Angel offered.

"That's what friends do," Shelly added.

Coral sighed. "I don't think I could start by swimming the tunnel," she said.

"You don't have to!" Angel cried. She took Coral's paw. "Let's go over here." She led them to an open part of the ocean. "There's plenty of room to flip here!"

Coral gulped. "What do I do first?"

Shelly and Angel took turns showing Coral how to do underwater flips. "Look at me!" Angel yowled. She flipped easily, over and over again.

"The trick is to swim as fast as you can before you start the flip," Shelly said. She swam into the open water and did a flawless flip. "That way you have the oomph to get all the way around."

Coral narrowed her eyes. She shook her tail out to get loose. Then she started to swim.

Shelly said to go fast, so Coral swam with all her might. Then she tucked her head down and threw her tail back, just like Angel and Shelly had shown her.

And she did it!

Coral was catching her breath when Angel and Shelly swam up to her. "That was purr-fect!" Angel cried.

"You got it on the first try!" Shelly added.

Coral couldn't believe it! "That wasn't scary," she said.

"Do you want to try again?" Angel asked.

Coral nodded. "Yes, I do!"

The girls swam through the clear blue water. They took turns doing flips. Soon Coral couldn't remember why she had ever been afraid. "This is so much fun!" she shouted.

"I need a break!" Angel said. She plopped down on a rock. "I'm just going to sit here for a minute."

"Good idea," Shelly said. She sat down next to Angel.

Coral was tired, too. There was no room left on that rock, so she looked around for someplace else to rest.

That's when she realized nothing looked familiar. "Hey!" she shouted. "Do you know where we are? Because this is definitely not Kittentail Cove!"

"What do you mean, this isn't Kittentail Cove?" Angel asked.

"We're not allowed to leave the cove!" Shelly cried. "Where are we?"

"I don't know," Coral moaned. She bit her lip. "I wasn't paying attention while we were swimming and flipping."

"Neither was I," Shelly groaned.

Angel looked worried. "We're going to

be in so much trouble!" she said. "How are we going to get home?"

If there were little butterfly fish fluttering in Coral's tummy earlier, now it felt like big blue whales! She couldn't remember ever being this nervous. "We need to stay calm!" she said. "We just need to look around. I'm sure we'll see something familiar soon. And then we'll hurry home!"

"Good plan," Shelly agreed. "Should we split up? That way we can see more of the ocean at once."

Angel shook her head. "I don't want to be alone out here! I think it's better for us to stay together."

For once, Coral agreed with Angel's plan. She nodded and said, "Come on. Let's try to retrace our swim."

The three purrmaids moved slowly through the water. They couldn't see Tortoiseshell Reef from where they were. All there was up ahead was a giant kelp forest.

Every moment they were lost made Coral worry more. *What are we going to do?* she thought.

Coral, Shelly, and Angel were very busy trying to find their way home. So they didn't notice the school of fish swimming toward them until they were surrounded by a hundred bright-green parrot fish.

Suddenly, Coral remembered something. "The South Canary Current!" she shouted. "Maybe these fish are headed there!"

Shelly's face lit up. "If we can find the South Canary Current . . ."

". . . it will take us home to Kittentail Cove!" Coral finished.

"You are so smart!" Angel applauded. "I knew there was nothing to worry about!"

Coral rolled her eyes. Angel had *definitely* been worried! "Let's follow those fish," she said.

There were so many parrot fish, they formed a green cloud. That made it easy to follow them without spooking them. Soon Shelly cried, "Look over there! It's the South Canary Current!"

A line of fish, turtles, and other sea creatures traveled in the flow of the South

Canary Current. It was like a high-speed highway for ocean folks. "We'll be home in no time!" Coral cheered. She started to swim toward the current.

But Angel grabbed Coral's paw. "Don't!" she yelled.

"Why?" Coral asked. "We have to go!"

Angel wouldn't let go. She pointed at the water in front of them. "Does that look like smooth sailing to you?"

Coral scowled. "I don't understand."

"Look closely," Angel urged.

"Is that a swarm of jellyfish up ahead?" Shelly gasped.

"I think it is," Angel said. Jellyfish were pretty harmless to purrmaids—unless they got stuck in a big group of them. One sting wasn't so bad, but getting stung over and over was not a good idea. "We can't go straight to the current."

"We have to find a way to go around them," Coral agreed.

"But they're everywhere," Shelly said. She was right. As the girls swam closer, they saw that the cloud of jellyfish stretched over most of the ocean. It was in front of them, from the top of the kelp forest almost to the surface of the water.

Angel pointed downward at the kelp forest. "If we can't go up, we'll go down."

Shelly shrugged. Coral frowned. But then they both nodded.

"I'll go first," Angel said. She swam toward the kelp. Shelly followed on her tail.

Coral hesitated. She was trying to be brave in front of her friends. But she felt nervous. *Who knew what was hiding in all that kelp?*

"Come on, Coral!" Shelly said.

"It's not so bad," Angel added. "Don't be a scaredy cat!"

Coral lowered her eyes. She didn't mean to be scared. She just liked doing things the safe way. The safe way never involved sharks or jellyfish or getting grounded. But now the safe way seemed to be through the forest. She gulped, then shouted, "I'm coming!"

The three friends entered the kelp forest together. There were a few natural passages that let them swim freely. But in other parts of the forest, the girls had to use their paws to part the kelp in order to get through.

"How do we know if we're going the right way?" Shelly asked.

Coral looked up. She tried to catch a glimpse of the South Canary Current, but all she could see was kelp. "I don't know," she answered.

"Let's keep moving," Angel suggested.

Coral nodded. She pushed aside a large kelp leaf. "Wow!" she cried.

"What is it?" Shelly asked. She shrank behind Angel. "Is it dangerous?"

Coral grinned. "No! It's the way out!" She held the kelp aside so her friends could swim through. They were back in the open ocean!

"Where's the current?" Angel looked around.

"It's up there!" Shelly said. "And I don't see any jellyfish, either!"

"Let's go!" Angel cried.

But Coral didn't move. She was staring at a trench in front of them. When she looked down, the water was darkened by shadows.

Coral thought something was lodged in the sand at the bottom of the trench. At first, it looked like a whale resting on the ocean floor. But then she realized it wasn't a living creature. "We've found a shipwreck!"

"I can't believe it!" Coral whispered. "I've read about shipwrecks. But I've never seen one!"

"That's because you never leave Kittentail Cove," Angel purred.

Coral scowled at Angel. But when she saw Angel's face, she knew her friend was kidding.

"Speaking of Kittentail Cove," Shelly said, "it's time for us to get back."

"I want to tell everyone at home about what we found!" Angel said.

"Wait!" Coral shouted. She gazed down at the shadowy ship. All afternoon, every time she had gotten scared, she had made herself be brave. If she could do it one more time, she and her friends could find something truly paw-some. "We have to explore the shipwreck first!"

Shelly's eyes grew wide, and Angel's jaw looked like it was going to fall off. "What did you say?" Angel sputtered.

"The South Canary Current will get us home in a flash," Coral said. "So I think we have a little bit of time. Just a quick look won't hurt, right?" She smiled. "Maybe we'll find something in the shipwreck to bring to school."

"That would be fin-tastic!" Angel said. She shrugged. "I guess I'm in!"

"Me too," Shelly said. "We won't get a chance like this again."

Coral started to swim down into the trench. Angel and Shelly swam beside her. "We can't explore for too long," she said.

"There's the Coral we know and love!" Shelly laughed.

"I'm serious!" Coral added. "We have to be home soon. I don't want to—"

"Get grounded," Angel said. "We know, we know."

Shelly elbowed Coral playfully. "We'll just take a quick peek." She flipped in the water, grinning. "This is so cool!"

The purrmaids swam closer to the ship. It had sunk down into the sand and was tipped over to one side. Giant barnacles covered the hull. Tattered bits of sail hung from the masts. There were holes scattered

around the deck. Beams of sunlight shone down to light different parts of the ship.

Coral peeked in a jagged hole to see into the ship's hold. A small fish swam out toward her. The hold was too dark to see very far. "This is scarier up close," she whispered.

"Do you want to go inside?" Angel asked.

Coral gulped. She didn't know if she could be brave enough to do that. But then she noticed a fancy door. It didn't look as creepy as the hold. She pointed. "Let's look there instead," she suggested.

All three girls had to yank on the handle to get it open.

"I hope this is worth it," Angel muttered.

Shelly peered through the door. "It's worth it!" she shouted, and raced ahead.

The room behind the door must have belonged to the captain of the ship. The floor and the walls were dotted with holes just like on the deck outside. Shelly swam straight to a large table nailed to the floor in the middle of the room. Angel studied the giant globe on one side of the room. Coral saw that the floor was littered with barrels, coils of rope, and tangles of seaweed. She took the lid off one of the barrels.

Something popped out and Coral squealed. "Yikes!"

Immediately, Angel and Shelly came to her side. "What happened?" Angel asked.

"That little guy scared me!" Coral said. A small crab scuttled away.

The girls giggled. Then Shelly said, "Come over here!" She led her friends back to the table. "Look what I found!" She held up a small golden tube. When she pulled on one end of the tube, it extended to be longer than Shelly's whole arm.

"What is it?" Angel asked.

"I think it's a spyglass," Shelly said.

Coral nodded. "Human sailors use these to see things far away," she said.

"I've never actually seen one," Shelly said.

"So it's purr-fect to show Ms. Harbor!" Angel grinned from ear to ear.

"One down, two to go!" Coral laughed. She put one paw around Angel's waist and the other around Shelly's. She hugged them tightly. "Let's see what else we can find!"

Angel's face lit up. "Actually, I have something to show you, too." She swam back to the globe.

Coral frowned. "Hey, Angel, you know that is way too heavy for us to carry home, right? Even if it wasn't nailed to the floor!"

"I know, Coral." Angel laughed. "I wasn't talking about the globe. I wanted to show you this." She held out her paw.

Coral swam closer to examine a small silver circle. She noticed a tiny needle under a glass cover, pointing at the letter N. "You found a compass!" she cried.

"It still works, too!" Angel turned around and waved the compass. She held it out again. The needle spun and pointed to N for north.

"It's paw-some, Angel," Shelly said.

"I'm bringing this to school tomorrow,"

Angel said. "That spyglass and this compass are purr-fect treasures from a shipwreck!"

Coral smiled, but she didn't feel completely happy. *Angel and Shelly found fabulous treasures to share with Ms. Harbor tomorrow,* she thought. *But I still have nothing. And it was* my *idea to come here in the first place. It's not fair!*

Shelly had the same thought. "Angel and I have our special things," she said. "We just need to find something for you, Coral."

Coral nodded. But there was nothing else in the captain's room that she could bring to school. Then she had an idea. "We still have the hold to search!" she cried. She pointed to a hole in the floor. "We can get down through here."

"I thought you said it was scary in there," Angel said.

Coral shrugged. "You keep saying not to be a scaredy cat. And we've been fine so far." She darted through the hole in the floor. "See if you two can keep up with me!"

7

The floor of the hold was covered in sand, sea-weed, and coral. It was like being in an under-water cave instead of a human ship. There were broken barrels scattered on the ground. Some sunlight filtered down from above.

Coral ignored all of that. She swam right to a half-open chest that was lit by a single sunbeam. "Over here!" she shouted.

"Wow!" Angel gasped. "Look at all these coins!"

Coral picked one up. "They're beautiful!" Purrmaids sometimes found one or two human coins around the ocean. But the girls had never seen this many in one place. "I'm going to bring a gold coin to school tomorrow!" she announced.

"That's a great idea!" Angel said.

Coral's cheeks hurt from grinning. *I'm so glad I was brave!* she thought. She squeezed the coin in her paw and said, "Let's get back to the South Canary Current. It's time to go home!"

The girls closed the lid of the chest and turned around to leave. Suddenly, the sunlight disappeared. "What happened to the sun?" Shelly asked.

Coral looked up. There was nothing blocking the holes in the deck. "It must have gotten cloudy," she answered.

"It's really dark now," Angel said. "I can't even see my tail!"

Coral scanned the darkened water. She pointed to a brighter spot in the darkness. "I think that's the hole we used to get down here. Let's head that way and see if we can get out."

The purrmaids dodged corals and sea sponges as they swam slowly toward the light. But Coral realized they weren't swimming toward sunlight. Sunlight wasn't green, and this light definitely was. This was more of a glow than a ray of light.

There were many harmless creatures in the ocean that glowed. Sea pens, krill, and lantern fish could all glow. Coral didn't think this was any of those things. None of them had sharp, scary teeth. But this thing did!

Coral hissed. "Quick! Hide!" She grabbed her friends' paws and pulled them behind a barrel. When they were hidden, she carefully peeked out to get a better look at the glowing creature.

The eerie green glow circled around the hold. It paused near the barrel. Now it was close enough for Coral to see its eyes.

"It looks like a monster!" Shelly whispered.

Coral bit her lip. "I think it's a shark," she said.

"A shark!" Angel gasped. "I knew we should have just gone home!"

Coral scowled. Angel was probably right. But they couldn't change that now. They had to think of some way to escape.

The trio huddled together. "The next time he moves away," Coral said, "we should swim as fast as we can!"

Shelly and Angel nodded. They watched the ghostly glow pass back and forth through the murky waters. Then it began to head toward the barrel. "What is he doing?" Angel gasped.

Coral panicked. *This is all my fault,* she thought. *We never should have come down to the hold.*

The shark paused at a giant sea fan. The glow from his skin cast creepy shadows on the ocean floor. That's when Coral saw her chance.

"Go, go, go!" she hissed.

Angel and Shelly raced away. Coral didn't follow them.

She knew they couldn't all outswim the shark. To make sure her friends were safe, Coral had to create a distraction.

She knew what she had to do.

Coral squared her shoulders. She popped up from behind the barrel and swam straight at the shark. When she got close, she tucked her head down and threw her tail back. Hopefully, the bubbles from her underwater flip would get the shark's attention.

It worked. He tilted his head toward her.

Shelly and Angel had reached a hole in the hold's wall. They just needed a little more time to get to safety. So Coral let go of her coin and waved her paws around while shouting, "Over here, Mr. Shark! Eat me if you want! But stay away from my friends!"

The green-glowing shark swam slowly in Coral's direction. She felt herself trembling.

But she had to be strong. She forced herself to look directly at the shark.

When they were eye to eye, though, Coral's courage faded away. She gulped.

The shark said, "Eat you? Why would I want to eat you?"

"You're—you're not here to eat me?" Coral stammered.

"Of course not!" the shark snapped.

"But you're a shark. That's what you do." Coral scratched her head. "Isn't it?"

"Catsharks always get a bad rap," he grumbled. "Everyone in the ocean thinks we're out to eat them!" He gestured at a stack of pale yellow pouches that hung from the sea fan. "I'm stuck here baby-sitting. These are my cousins. My mom and my aunt went to get a bite to eat."

Coral's eyes grew wide. The shark saw that she was scared, so he shouted, "Worms! We eat worms! Or tiny fish! Or shrimp!"

Coral exhaled with relief. "I didn't know you weren't a purrmaid-eating type of shark," she admitted.

"Well, you're not the only one." The shark sighed. "Why do you think we live inside a shipwreck? Nobody wants us around. Everyone says we're too danger-ous." He swam back to the sea fan. "No one even bothers to get to know us."

Coral felt awful. She didn't know any-thing about catsharks.

She swam to his side. "I'm Coral," she said. "I'm a purrmaid from Kittentail Cove."

"I'm Chomp," he answered. "I'm from right here."

Coral giggled. "It's nice to meet you, Chomp."

"What are you doing down here inside the shipwreck?" Chomp asked. "And the two purrmaids who swam away—were those your friends?"

Coral nodded. "My best friends, actually. We were trying to find the South Canary Current. Then we saw the shipwreck, and we wanted to explore."

"It's a pretty cool place to live," Chomp said.

"It really is!" Coral agreed. "But it's time for us to get home."

"Come and visit again sometime," Chomp said.

"And you should come visit me, too!" Coral suggested. "All you have to do is ride the South Canary Current. It will bring you directly to the entrance of Kittentail Cove."

"I'll remember that!" Chomp answered. He waved goodbye.

By the time Coral swam out of the shipwreck, she was grinning from ear to ear. It had been an exciting day!

Then Angel's voice startled her. "Coral! You're alive!"

Shelly and Angel hurried over to their friend's side. "We thought you were right behind us,"

Shelly said. "When we got out and you weren't here . . . we didn't know what to do!"

"We were so scared!" Angel added.

"I didn't mean to scare you," Coral said. "I wanted to give you more time to get away. But I didn't need to do that!"

"What happened with the monster?" Shelly asked.

"He isn't a monster!" Coral explained.

"He's a catshark, and catsharks don't eat purrmaids."

"What a relief!" Shelly said.

"I think there's been enough adventure today," Angel purred. "Let's get to the current so we can go home."

The purrmaids hurried up to the South Canary Current. It was as crowded as Angel's mother had warned it would be.

From time to time, they got bumped by turtles, fish, and even other purrmaids. The girls stayed close together and kept an eye on each other.

When they took the exit to Kittentail Cove and swam through the gates of the town, Coral glanced up at the clock tower. "We made it!" she cried. "It isn't dinnertime yet!"

"That means we won't get grounded," Angel laughed, "*and* we found the coolest treasures to bring to school tomorrow!"

Coral froze. Her gold coin! "Oh no!" she moaned. "I don't have my treasure!"

"What do you mean?" Shelly asked.

"I must have dropped my coin at the shipwreck!" Coral said. "When I was trying to get Chomp's attention, I started waving my paws around." She looked down at her tail. "I think I let go of it then."

Angel and Shelly glanced at each other.

"You can have my treasure," Shelly offered.

"Or mine," Angel added.

Coral shook her head. "It's really nice of you to say that," she said. "But I can't take your stuff! That wouldn't be fair." She sighed. "It's my fault I lost the coin. I'll just bring in that shell from my collection."

Coral tried to cheer up as they swam home. But when they reached Leondra's Square, she was still feeling down. Her friends each gave her a hug when they said goodbye, but even that didn't help.

"We'll see you here tomorrow?" Angel asked.

Coral nodded. "Of course."

"Smile, Coral," Shelly said. "Things will be better tomorrow, I'm sure."

Coral tried to smile for Shelly. But in her heart, she was thinking, *They couldn't get any worse.*

Coral hardly slept that night. She tossed and turned on her oyster-shell bed for hours.

She knew she was running behind because she was moving so slowly. But when she got to Leondra's Square to meet up with Angel and Shelly, she realized how late she was. Not only was Shelly already waiting, but Angel was there, too!

"Sorry I'm a little slow today," Coral said.

"Don't worry!" Angel answered. Shelly and Angel exchanged a glance. They had huge grins on their faces.

"Let's get to school," Shelly suggested. "We have our treasures now!"

Coral bit her lip. It was nice to see Angel and Shelly so excited about the treasures they found in the shipwreck. It wasn't their fault that Coral had lost hers. She forced herself to smile and swam alongside her friends.

As the students arrived in Eel-Twelve, Ms. Harbor welcomed them. "I hope you all brought something to share," she said. The students nodded. Ms. Harbor smiled. "I can't wait to see your treasures and begin getting to know all of you."

"Can I go first?" Baker asked.

"No, me!" Taylor shouted.

"Everyone will get a turn, I purr-omise," Ms. Harbor said.

Ms. Harbor called up one purrmaid at a time to present a treasure. Coral did her best to pay attention, but she kept thinking about the gold coin. *I can't believe I lost it,* she thought. *It would have been so purr-fect for today!*

Coral didn't notice it was Angel's turn until Shelly tapped her shoulder. She looked up and saw that Angel was floating in the front of the classroom.

"Shelly and I will present together," Angel announced. She winked at Coral.

Of course they're presenting as a team, Coral thought. *The spyglass and compass go together.*

Shelly tugged on Coral's paw. "Come on, Coral," she said.

Coral shook her head. "I don't have my

coin," she whispered. "My treasure doesn't match yours!"

"You're wrong!" Shelly said. She dragged Coral to float next to Angel.

"There are many things in the ocean that are special to Shelly and me," Angel said. "But nothing is more special than family and friends."

"We're both really lucky to have fin-tastic families," Shelly continued. "But the treasure Angel and I want to share today is our best friend, Coral."

All eyes turned to Coral. She didn't understand what was going on. Angel didn't give her a chance to ask any questions. "Yesterday, we learned that the most special things in the world are the ones we hold close to our hearts," Angel said.

"Sometimes Coral can be extra careful," Shelly continued, "and that can make some purrmaids think she's a scaredy cat."

"But she's not!" Angel said. "She's actually one of the bravest purrmaids I know."

"She's only cautious because she cares so much about her friends," Shelly added. "Coral would do anything for us, and we would do anything for her."

"There is nothing closer to our hearts

than our best friend," Angel said.

"What a wonderful presentation!" Ms. Harbor cried. "Well done, Shelly and Angel!"

Coral could feel her face getting hot. "I treasure you two, as well," she said, and the whole class cheered.

Coral was very quiet as she swam out to recess. She was speechless after Shelly and Angel's presentation. They had made her feel so loved and special. She couldn't believe how lucky she was to have such good friends.

Angel and Shelly weren't sure why Coral was so quiet. "Did we do something wrong?" Shelly asked.

"We were trying to be nice," Angel added.

"No, no, no!" Coral cried. She rushed forward to hug her friends. "That was one of the nicest things anyone has ever done for me!"

Shelly and Angel beamed. But the moment was interrupted when the girls heard their classmate Taylor scream, "A shark!"

"He's coming for us!" Baker shouted. "Swim for your lives!"

Coral whipped around to see what was happening. That's when she saw someone familiar.

The other purrmaids cowered behind the rock benches in the schoolyard. Ms. Harbor swam toward the shark, ready to protect her students. Coral darted forward and put herself between the shark and Ms. Harbor. "Chomp!" she shouted. "What are you doing here?"

Chomp grinned, and all of his teeth were on display. That caused a new chorus of screams from Coral's classmates.

"Get away, Coral! He'll eat you!" Taylor yelled.

Coral turned around and shook her head. "No, he won't," she replied. She motioned for the purrmaids to stop hiding. Angel and Shelly gulped, but they swam out from behind the benches. The rest of her classmates poked their heads out but didn't come forward.

Coral said, "Ms. Harbor, I'd like to introduce you to someone—my new friend, Chomp."

Ms. Harbor opened and closed her mouth like a fish. But she didn't make a sound. Chomp gave her a toothy grin and extended his fin. Coral nodded at her teacher. Ms. Harbor finally put her paw out so they could shake.

"Chomp is a catshark," Coral continued, "and yesterday, I learned a lot." She winked at Shelly and Angel. "My best friends helped me learn that I don't have to be a scaredy cat about new things." She smiled at Chomp. "And Chomp taught me that catsharks aren't dangerous. They are just misunderstood."

"Really?" Baker asked.

"Really," Chomp answered. "I didn't come to Kittentail Cove for lunch! I came to give this to Coral." He held out a small package wrapped in seaweed.

"What is that?" Ms. Harbor asked.

Chomp grinned again. "Coral isn't the only one who learned something," he explained. "She taught me there are other good fish in the sea. You just have to be willing to give them a chance, and maybe you'll make a new friend."

Coral unwrapped the package. Inside were three gold coins from the shipwreck!

"After you left," Chomp said, "I realized you dropped your coin. I wanted to bring it to you so you'd always remember me." He giggled. "I brought some extras—for your two friends. And I added some hooks so you can attach them to your bracelets. That way you won't lose them!"

Once again, Coral was speechless.

"How fin-tastic!" Ms. Harbor cheered. "Thank you both for teaching us about catsharks. And thank you for visiting, Chomp, and for introducing him, Coral. What a purr-fect thing to share with the class—a new friend!"

The entire class cheered. Coral gave Chomp a big hug. The other purrmaids swam up to him and started asking questions. Coral pulled Angel and Shelly aside. She held out a gold coin to each of them.

"But Chomp gave those to you!" Angel said.

Coral shook her head. "He wanted us each to have a coin. We can put them on our bracelets to remind us to be brave."

"That is a paw-some plan!" Shelly cried.

Coral put her gold coin on her bracelet. She smiled and purred, "I can't wait for our next adventure!"